THE CROSS AND THE FLAME

While the Great Plague rages through London, Hester dreams of her sailor sweetheart Jonathan, despite being promised in marriage to her father's friend — the odious Thomas Latham. The deaths of her mother and baby brother bring guilty relief when the wedding is postponed. Then Jonathan returns to the news that Hester has died in the plague. Will he discover the deception before she is forced to marry a man who has no place in her heart?

Books by Roberta Grieve
in the Linford Romance Library:

A HATFUL OF DREAMS
THE COMFORT OF STRANGERS

ROBERTA GRIEVE

THE CROSS AND THE FLAME

Complete and Unabridged

LINFORD
Leicester

First published in Great Britain in 2005

First Linford Edition
published 2008

British Library CIP Data

Grieve, Roberta
　　The cross and the flame.—Large print ed.—
Linford romance library
　　1. Forced marriage—Fiction 2. Great Plague,
London, England, *1664 – 1666*—Fiction
　　3. Historical fiction 4. Large type books
　　I. Title
　　823.9′2 [F]

ISBN 978–1–84782–148–5

Published by
F. A. Thorpe (Publishing)
Anstey, Leicestershire

Set by Words & Graphics Ltd.
Anstey, Leicestershire
Printed and bound in Great Britain by
T. J. International Ltd., Padstow, Cornwall

This book is printed on acid-free paper

1

The swiftly ebbing tide hissed and sucked at the piers of London Bridge, leaving behind a gleaming expanse of wet mud on either side of the river. Wherries and lighters, ferryboats and merchant ships vied for position as they tied up for the night at the wharves and piers along the riverbank.

Hester Wright gazed out of the window, her needlework unheeded in her lap. She never tired of watching the busy scene from her window-seat in the old house on London Bridge, although she seldom had time to sit idle. Today, however, she could not settle to anything as she anxiously awaited the ship that would bring Jonathan home. The *Caroline* was due back from her three-month voyage any day now.

As the sun crept down the sky, the long shadows of the houses on the bridge began to eclipse the streaks of gold and red that coloured the Thames. Night was falling fast, but it brought no relief from the unseasonable heat of that late spring in 1665.

It was time to light the lamps and prepare for her father's homecoming. Master Wright liked his supper on the table after a hard day at the workshop. Hester knew that she should be tending to the household, not dreaming at the window, but still she lingered, although common sense told her that he would not come today. The *Caroline* had probably berthed farther downriver at Gravesend or Greenwich and would come upstream on the morning tide.

'Come away, Hester. Your father and the 'prentices will soon be home for their supper.' The soft, tired voice of her mother, recalled her to her duties.

Elizabeth Wright's pregnancy had been difficult from the start and there were fears that she would lose the child, as she had six others in recent years. Hester knew that her mother bore her discomfort bravely in her longing to give Charles the son he wanted.

With a last lingering look downriver, Hester left her needlework on the window seat and went to where her mother lay in her bed, in the corner of the large room where the family ate and took their leisure. Although almost too weak to move, Elizabeth liked to be able to keep an eye on the comings and goings of the household, protesting that from her chamber at the top of the tall, narrow house she felt cut off from everybody.

'Dearest Mother, forgive me. I was lost in thought. Here, let me make you comfortable.' Hester cooled Elizabeth's forehead with a damp cloth and straightened the rumpled sheets, propping her up on the pillows. She put thoughts of Jonathan out of her mind, not wishing to trouble her mother with her anxieties.

Elizabeth's bed was set in a corner of the large room, under the window which looked out on to the narrow street that ran down the middle of the bridge. From here she could watch the comings and goings of her neighbours, a pastime which diverted her mind from the pain and discomfort of her difficult pregnancy. Today though, wearied with the heat, she had dozed the hours away.

When she felt well enough, she would sit by the door in the sunshine, or on the window seat at the other end of the room looking out over the busy river. But the unusually long spell of hot weather had left her weak and lethargic and, in the past few days, she had taken to her bed in earnest.

Now she roused herself to smile at her daughter. 'Dreaming of your handsome cousin I dare say?'

Hester felt the hot colour washing over her face. 'I confess I was thinking about Jonathan. His mother must worry so when he is delayed. I just pray he is safe.'

'We all pray for him. These are troubling times.' A shadow passed

4

across Elizabeth's face as she recalled the family's changing fortunes over the past few months. 'I had thought things would improve with the return of the King. Yet he sports and plays while the Dutch make havoc with our ships in the Channel. And I fear your father has over-reached himself with his new workshop. What use for him to make fine leather goods for the nobility when they refuse to pay their bills?' Her hands plucked restlessly at the sheet which covered her swollen belly.

Hester leaned over and brushed the damp hair from her mother's brow. 'Don't fret, Mother. I am sure my father knows what he's about.' She turned from the bed. 'Now I must see what Nellie has for our supper.'

In the kitchen, Hester found Nellie the maid sitting in a corner by the fire, her sacking apron over her face, her hair straggling damply across her shoulders. The smell of cooking told her that at least the girl had set the beef to cook before giving in to whatever ailed her.

I suppose she's quarrelled with Dan or Will and we shall have long faces at the supper table tonight, Hester thought. She had suspected for some time that the maid was sweet on one of her father's apprentices. The girl was always looking for excuses to visit the workshop and was quick to offer if errands needed to be done in the vicinity of Cheapside.

But it was not a lover's tiff that had upset Nellie. She lifted her head and began to wait. 'Oh Miss Hester, Lord have mercy on us. I fear the plague is upon us, oh mercy me.' She covered her face with the apron again and sobbed anew.

'What nonsense is this, Nellie?' Hester asked, removing the joint of beef and setting it on a wooden platter on the table, where it sizzled and spat in its juices, filling the air with a delicious aroma.

But Hester's appetite vanished when she heard what Nellie had to say. 'Tis true, Miss. When I took the Master his bread and cheese, I heard the 'prentices talking about it.'

A tiny frisson of fear ran through her, but she forced herself to remain calm for the girl's sake. After all, there were some few cases of plague every year, especially during the hot weather. And she, too, had heard of the deaths in the parish of St Giles some weeks before. But there had been no real outbreak during her lifetime, she thought, although she recalled tales of a bad epidemic the year before she was born. Surely such a visitation could not happen again.

Nellie, still sobbing behind her apron, rocked on the stool. 'I'm afeared I've caught it, Miss. I'm that hot and giddy that I had to sit down and rest when I got home.' And the little maid broke out into a fresh storm of weeping.

Hester moved to comfort her, then hesitated. Suppose Nellie had brought the plague home with her? Everyone knew how easy it was to pass on to others. And the girl certainly looked ill with her flushed cheeks and bright eyes. But if she were ill she would have to be nursed.

The Wrights would never turn her out on the streets, whatever their fears of becoming infected.

Chiding herself for her selfish thoughts, Hester gently smoothed the tangled hair away from the maid's perspiring face. 'Come along, Nellie. Of course you feel hot and giddy. It's such a hot day, and you've been sitting here by the fire for hours. Come away and let me bathe your face. You'll soon feel better.'

Nellie allowed herself to be led over to the wooden bucket which stood on the rough table under the window. Hester dipped a cloth into the water and bathed the girl's face, smoothing her hair gently back from her flushed cheeks and straightening her mobcap. Then she filled a pewter mug with water from the other pail. As she tended to the maid she checked carefully for signs of the plague, although she knew that sometimes the dreaded buboes did not appear until some days after the onset of illness.

Relieved to discover nothing, she took a deep breath and spoke briskly to mask her concern. 'Now, what's all this nonsense about the plague, Nellie? Where did you get hold of such an idea?'

Nellie took a deep draught of the cool water and spoke more calmly now. 'I was taking the Master a bite to eat, seeing as he's been working all hours getting those fancy boots made for his Lordship. As I left the workshop I stopped to talk to Dan.'

Hester hid a smile. She might have known. Will was far too quiet to attract a girl like Nellie. Dan was a cheerful, open-faced youth, who worked hard and had the makings of a good leather-worker. She hoped he wasn't leading poor Nellie on.

'I heard them talking about the plague, and Dan told me there's more cases now, even been some in Allhallows parish. He said there's talk that everyone in London will be afflicted before the summer's out,' Nellie told her.

Despite the worry Nellie's words aroused, Hester tried to reassure the other girl, while silently praying that she was right.

'I expect he was teasing you. The apprentices are great ones for playing jokes. You mustn't take note of what they say,' Hester said. 'Besides, Allhallows is still far enough away for us not to worry about it. We're safe here.' She patted the girl's shoulder and continued. 'Now, stop fretting and get on with you. Mama expected supper ready long since and my father will be home soon.'

Nellie rubbed her hand across her eyes and tried a watery smile. 'I'm sorry I got all in a fret, Miss Hester. It was just thinking about the plague. It brought it all back to me you see.'

Hester smiled sympathetically, remembering that the girl had been orphaned in the last outbreak. She had escaped the infection but the experience had left its mark on her.

'We'll look after you, Nellie,' Hester said and started to carry the dishes through to the living-room, glad to escape from the heat of the kitchen.

The maid, comforted by her mistress's calm demeanour, made haste to follow with the platter of beef, suddenly remembering how stern Master Wright could be when displeased.

As they entered the big living-room, the street door opened and Jonathan's mother, Mary Blake, came in. She was a tall woman with blue eyes like her son's and fair hair, covered now with a white lace cap. When she smiled there were traces of the carefree young wife she had once been, but for the present her expression was solemn as she returned from one of her visits to the sick and needy of the parish.

Hester wished now that she'd accompanied her as she usually did, instead of pining at the window. Jonathan's return would not be hastened by her sitting and wishing it so. Tomorrow, she decided, Nellie could look after her mother and she would go with Mary. Like her aunt, she took little heed of the risk of infection, having noticed that those who seemed most fearful were the very ones who succumbed. Besides, she liked to feel useful and the time would pass all the more quickly for being busy.

Noting her aunt's serious demeanour, however, Hester thought maybe Nellie was right to be worried after all and perhaps the plague was spreading. She was about to question the older woman but decided to wait until they were alone so as not to alarm her mother. Elizabeth sanctioned her visits to the poor in normal times, but would be reluctant to let her go if the plague had its hold on the whole city. Instead she spoke cheerfully.

'Supper is almost ready, Aunt. Here let me take your basket.'

As she spoke Charles Wright returned from his workshop in Cheapside with the two apprentices. Her smile of welcome for them died on her lips when she realised they were not alone. Behind them loomed the burly figure of Thomas Latham.

Now why has Father brought him here, she thought with a flicker of irritation, mingled with uneasiness? Try as she might she could find nothing to like about her father's friend and business associate. Big and beefy, with a red face, a nose threaded with broken veins, and a low forehead almost eclipsed by the black curly wig, he affected in the manner of the Court, Thomas was not an attractive man. Besides, she blamed him for the change in their fortunes.

Perhaps he's here on account of Mary, Hester thought Her mother's cousin had been widowed when Jonathan was a child. She had since made her home with the Wrights and had always seemed content with her lot. Yet I suppose it is only natural that she should think of remarrying, but surely she could do better than Master Latham, for all his wealth and fine house by the river, Hester thought. Thomas Latham was a rich merchant who, besides owning many ships, had his fingers in all sorts of money-making pies. Since the return of the King some years before and the setting up of the court in London, Thomas seemed to prosper day by day. The big house in Thames Street was flanked by huge warehouses, which backed on to the river. Here his ships would offload their precious cargo of Chinese silks and Indian carpets, French furnishings and other costly goods.

With the increasing prosperity of the capital, it had become the fashion for the city's burghers and tradesmen to ape the ways of the court and nobility. Thomas boasted that he could sell his goods thrice over and could not get enough of them to satisfy the demand.

Hester shuddered with dislike as he came into the room. She avoided his eyes, greeting her father and the two apprentices.

Charles crossed the room to kiss his wife, saying, 'I have brought Thomas home for supper. He finds it lonely

14

dining by himself night after night in that great house of his.' He turned to Hester. 'Set a place for our guest, Daughter. Nellie, fetch wine.'

Thomas came into the room, sweeping off his plumed hat, and bowing over Elizabeth's hand. ''Tis good of you to welcome a lonely widower, Mistress Wright, especially when, as I see, you are not in the best of health.'

Elizabeth smiled a welcome and settled back on her pillows exhausted. As Hester came back into the room, Thomas came towards her, stepping closer than she would have liked. 'The daughter of the house grows comelier each time I see her, Master Wright,' he said with a laugh. His words were directed to his friend, but his hot eyes swept over her. She shrank back from the expression in them, shuddering inwardly and moving round to the other side of the table.

Why is my father friendly with such a man? Hester wondered, as she replaced the pewter tankards with fine crystal goblets and helped Nellie to serve the food. When their plates were filled she sat down to her own meal, taking her place between Dan and Will, anxious to put as much distance between herself and their guest as possible.

Master Latham was putting himself out to be agreeable to everyone tonight, she thought, as Mary laughed in reply to one of his remarks. Perhaps he was courting her after all.

She put the disagreeable thought out of her mind and turned to Dan. In a low voice, she gently admonished him for upsetting Nellie that afternoon.

'I didn't mean for her to take fright,' the lad replied indignantly. ''Tis true what I told her, isn't that so, Will?' He looked to his fellow apprentice for support and Will nodded, tearing a piece of bread to mop up his gravy.

After a quick glance at Master Wright, Dan said quietly, 'I'm truly sorry, Miss. The master did tell us not to speak of it. But I wanted to warn Nellie not to linger in the market in case she should pick up the infection.'

'Don't worry, Dan. I'm sure it is just a rumour. Whenever there are one or two cases, the numbers are exaggerated as the news passes from mouth to mouth. I'm sure it is nothing like as bad as you fear,' Hester said.

Nellie came in from the kitchen bringing more wine and Hester smiled as she saw the look that passed between the maid and the apprentice. Nellie had clearly forgiven Dan for his earlier teasing. Recognising the signs of dawning love between the young couple turned her thoughts to Jonathan once more.

If he were here at table with us I would not care who else was present, even Master Latham, she thought. My happiness would be complete. Her cheeks flushed in anticipation of his return and their imminent betrothal.

Thomas must have noticed for he leaned across the table towards her. 'What thoughts cause a young maiden to blush so prettily?' he asked with a leer. When she did not reply, he laughed and lifted his glass to his lips, murmuring something to her father.

Hester kept her eyes lowered demurely and tried to concentrate on her food. She would ignore him. His flowery compliments meant nothing to her.

One would think he were at the King's table where such manners are accepted, she thought, rather than in the home of a God-fearing, hard-working family. And why does my father not reprimand him for his forward ways, she asked herself.

But Charles appeared not to notice anything untoward in his guest's manners, or that his daughter was uneasy in the man's presence.

Finally Hester could bear it no more and asked permission to leave the table. She sat beside her mother, trying to coax her to eat. As the evening wore on, the two men drank more and more wine and the conversation became loud and heated. Inevitably the talk turned to the rumours of plague and to

Hester's dismay, Thomas repeated what Nellie had said earlier. The increase in the number of cases had been confirmed. He had seen it himself on the mortality bills posted in the parish.

'I am of a mind to leave the city if things should continue thus,' he said. 'I will stay at my house in the country until all danger from the distemper has passed.'

Nellie, clearing the supper things away, started to wail, rushing out of the room in some distress. Dan excused himself from the table and followed her.

'Now, Master Latham, you have set my poor maid in a dither, the 'prentices too. I have spent half the day trying to reassure them that things are not as bad as they fear.'

'Your pardon, Mister Wright. I had thought that all in London were aware of the situation by now.'

Charles gave his friend a stern look. 'I think it best we do not talk of it before the women,' he said. 'Besides there are always a few cases, especially when the weather is as hot and humid as it has been. What does one or two deaths signify? 'Tis not an epidemic by a long way, nor will be, I am sure.'

Hester, watching her father's face closely, was not convinced. He's trying to set our minds at ease, she thought, turning to her mother and noting with relief that she seemed not to have heard.

But Mary spoke up then. 'It may not yet be an epidemic,' she said in a low voice, with a quick glance towards the bed where her cousin lay with eyes now closed. 'But Master Latham speaks truly. There are more cases every day. I have seen with my own eyes how quickly it strikes. As you know, I work among the poor of the parish and it seems to afflict them more readily.' She smiled reassuringly and continued. 'But I think, so long as we take all the necessary precautions, we will be safe enough.'

Hester was comforted by her aunt's words. After all, Mary moved freely between their house and the hovels of the poor, and she never took ill.

'What precautions can we take if the distemper rages through the city as it has done in earlier times?' Thomas asked.

Hester noted with scorn how Thomas' hand shook as he drained his glass hastily, before heaving himself to his feet. He's afraid, she thought.

Mary smiled. 'Never fear, Master Latham, as I said it is only the poor, crowded together in their noisome hovels who fall victim in their hordes. And a fine gentleman such as yourself has no need to frequent such places.'

'Just so, Mistress Blake, just so,' Thomas said, bowing to the assembled company and taking up his plumed hat. 'However I am resolved that tomorrow I will make arrangements for securing my warehouses against theft. I will leave for my house in the country by the week's end.'

He crossed the room, a little unsteady from the wine he had drunk, to where Hester sat on a stool at her mother's bedside.

'Goodnight, Mistress Wright. I thank you for your hospitality.' He spoke to Elizabeth but his hot little eyes were on Hester. She whispered her farewell, her eyes downcast. He chuckled and turned away.

At the door he paused. 'I advise you to leave the city also, Master Wright,' he said. 'If only for the sake of your lady wife and your sweet daughter.'

'There is no need for such haste,' Charles assured him. 'Besides, I cannot leave my workshops untended. And there are still orders to be filled. Unlike you, I cannot afford to lose trade.'

'If you will not go yourself, at least allow your wife and daughter to be my guests,' Thomas said.

Hester sighed with relief when her father declined the offer. 'I believe you are reacting somewhat hastily, my friend,' he said. 'Besides, my wife is in no condition to make such a journey. However, I thank you for your kind thought.'

Thomas shrugged as if the matter were of no importance. 'Goodnight then, Master Wright. Do not forget what we spoke of. I shall expect all to be arranged when next we meet.'

'It shall be, Master Latham. You can depend on it,' Charles replied.

Hester was puzzled. Surely her father had said that they would not leave London. But what other arrangements could they be speaking of? Her father had declared adamantly that, despite their friendship, he would do no more business with Master Latham after his last disastrous venture. She hoped he had not changed his mind and was contemplating further risks in an attempt to recoup the losses of the previous year.

The supper things were put away and Nellie, reassured at last that she was in no immediate danger from the plague, had retired to her attic chamber. Dan and Will had also said their goodnights and gone to their bed in the little room behind the old workshop where the apprentices had always slept.

Hester settled her mother for the night and took up her candle, ready to go to her own chamber. But Charles beckoned her to sit once more at the table and sat down opposite her, his face grave. She dutifully gave him her attention, thinking he would speak of the precautions to be taken against infection should the plague break out in their parish. However, his next words took her by surprise.

'Hester, my dear, I have been thinking that it is high time you were wed. Most girls of your age already have a husband, or are at least betrothed.'

'But Father, I have no wish to marry,' Hester said, blushing at the lie. She would marry Jonathan tomorrow if it were possible. But she could not say so until he had spoken to her father as he had promised. Besides, he had no fortune and no hope of being able to support a wife for many a year. Charles would need to be persuaded that it would be a suitable match.

Hester had planned to seek her mother's help in preparing her father for Jonathan's declaration. Elizabeth had often declared that she had married Charles for love. But since her illness, Hester had felt it wrong to burden her mother with such concerns.

'Whether you wish it or not, you must wed. You are seventeen years old and arrangements must be made within the next year or so,' Charles said. 'What will become of you when I am no longer here? I had hoped to leave my family well provided for, but as you know I have had much misfortune in business lately. You must have a husband to support you.' He smiled earnestly. 'I only want what every father should want for a beloved daughter.'

Then let me marry Jonathan, fortune or not, Hester thought. But she did not speak her thoughts aloud. Instead she returned the pressure of her father's hand.

'Dearest Father, do not speak of

leaving us. You are a fit man, in your prime. You will be with us for many a long year, God willing. It is this talk of the plague which has distressed you, I am sure,' she said.

'No, Daughter. It has been in my mind to settle this for many a month. I wish to see you safely cared for, in case something should happen to me.'

He let go her hand and stood up, pacing the room while Hester looked on apprehensively. She suddenly felt she knew what his next words would be. Even so she could hardly believe it when he said abruptly, 'Master Latham has asked for your hand.'

Hester gasped but he ignored her and continued, 'He is a good man, rich too, well able to provide for you in the manner I would wish. If you marry straight away, you would be safe were the plague to sweep the city as has been predicted. He will take you to his house in the country, away from danger of infection.'

'How could I leave you and Mother?' Hester protested. But it was no use. She could see that his mind was made up. Not yet, she silently pleaded. Please give me time, time for Jonathan to come back and stake his claim. 'Father, please — ' she gasped.

But he carried on speaking, 'Master Latham asks for no dowry.' He took her hands in his. 'Dearest Daughter, you cannot imagine what a weight has been lifted from my mind. Through my own foolishness I speculated and lost my fortune, which was to have been your dowry. It has vexed me for months that you would not be able to make a good match — and all through my own fault.'

Hester had always been a dutiful daughter. If she had not fallen in love with Jonathan it would never have crossed her mind to defy her father.

But at the thought of Thomas Latham's hard eyes, buried in rolls of fat, gleaming like pebbles as they looked her up and down, she shuddered. In her mind's eye she pictured his moist lips as he ran his tongue over them.

I would rather die than marry him, she thought.

2

The next day, a neighbour brought news of more cases of the plague and Nellie started to cry again, refusing to go to the market even when threatened with dismissal.

'Let me stay and tend the mistress,' she begged. And soft-hearted Hester gave in and went for the provisions herself.

Mary, on her way to visit the sick family she had been tending, accompanied Hester part of the way. The busy streets rang with the sound of cart-wheels on the cobbles, mingled with the shouts of the street vendors. It was another hot day and stench of rotting vegetation was almost overpowering.

Since her mother's illness, Hester had not ventured far from home and she had become used to the breeze which wafted through the open windows, bringing a welcome coolness off the river.

As they hurried through the crowded streets, Hester couldn't help wondering how many of those they passed carried the seeds of plague. She fingered the posy of dried flowers, dusty and crumbling now, which hung at her waist. She wasn't sure she believed in the power of the herbs to protect her from illness, although she knew that many people set great store by them.

She had only kept them as a reminder of Jonathan, who had given her the posy of lavender, valerian and tormentil before he left on his last voyage. Now she wondered whether they really would prove a safeguard against the plague.

She recalled Jonathan's tender words as he presented the posy to her. 'These herbs will protect you from ague and distemper, so I've been told,' he said. He related how an old woman, who claimed to be a soothsayer, as well as a herbalist, had pressed them on him when the ship docked at Greenwich. 'If you are going into the city you will have need of them,' she'd told him. 'The plague is rife in London town.'

Jonathan, in terror lest any harm had befallen Hester, had hurried home to the old house on London Bridge. 'I could not bear it if anything happened to you,' he'd said, his passionate outburst revealing his feelings for her.

Charles had hastened to reassure him. ''Tis true, there have been a few cases of the distemper but they are mainly in the poorer parts of the city. There have been none so far in this parish. I am sure there is nothing to worry about. You may go off on your next voyage with an easy mind. I shall make sure your mother and my family take no unnecessary risks,' he said.

Hester too had calmed his fears, and had said her farewells with a smile shining through her tears as he boarded the *Caroline*. But that had been six months ago.

While he had been away, the weather had turned much warmer, bringing with it an increasing number of plague victims. But that was the least of her worries. She was far more concerned about the continuing war with Holland, despite the news of a naval victory earlier in the month. English merchantmen had been a prey to warships, as well as Dutch privateers, for many months.

After the loss of her father's investment, Hester was well aware of the risks to shipping and prayed constantly for Jonathan's safety. Good seamanship and fair weather were often no match for the determined efforts of those who would plunder the richly laden vessels, which plied the English Channel.

'Please God, keep the *Caroline* safe and all who sail in her,' she whispered now, fingering the posy once more.

Mary saw the action and smiled. 'You are fearful for my son,' she said. 'But there are many reasons why a ship may be delayed.'

They reached the row of market stalls which lined the narrow street and Mary paused. 'I know you and Jonathan are fond of each other. But Master Wright has told me of his plans for your future. It would not be wise for you to become too close to my son.'

Hester lowered her gaze, afraid that her aunt would read her feelings. She had hoped that Mary would be an ally in her appeal to her father. In any case, the warning had come too late. Hester was in love with Jonathan and he with her.

Mary turned into an alleyway lined with dark hovels and Hester carried on into the market. As she filled her basket with fruit and vegetables brought in from the surrounding countryside, her mind was not on her task. Her prayers for Jonathan's return were now more fervent than they had been the day before. If, as he hoped, he had been offered the position of mate of the *Caroline* he would be in a position to offer for her hand in marriage. Although Jonathan was still young, he had proved his worth on many voyages, and the captain desired to show his appreciation of his hard work.

He'll be captain of his own ship before long, Hester told herself, and then we will be able to marry.

Before he'd left on this last voyage, he had declared his love for her, promising that on his return he would speak to her father.

'I know it may be many years before we can wed, but I shall be able to leave you with an easy mind if we are betrothed. And how can your father refuse when he hears of my advancement?' he'd said, kissing her tenderly.

Despite the fact that they were cousins once removed, Hester was sure that Master Wright would consent to the match. After all, he was fond of Jonathan, who had joined their household as a child along with his widowed mother, Mary. And he had always encouraged the friendship between his daughter and her cousin as they grew up together.

And is he not also a doting father who has seldom denied me anything I wished? Hester thought smiling. The smile faded as she reflected on her family's changed fortunes in the past months.

Her father, at the instigation of his friend Thomas Latham, had invested much of his hard-earned wealth in cargo from the Indies. Then the ship had been seized in the Channel by a Dutch privateer and everything was lost. It had not affected Master Latham for he was a rich man, but Charles Wright had felt the loss keenly.

They were not yet paupers by a long way, Hester thought, for Father still had his thriving business in a street off Cheapside, where he made soft boots and other leather goods for the nobility. But she knew he was worried by the change in their fortunes, and had even begun to speak of giving up the large workshop where he employed several journeymen as well as two apprentices.

As she wandered through the market place, Hester's head filled with dreams of Jonathan, she couldn't help overhearing the gossip of the stallholders.

'Plague,' was the word on everyone's lips and she gave a little shudder, drawing her cloak around her as if it would protect her from contagion.

'I hear the King and all his court have fled to Oxford,' the poulterer said, deftly plucking a fat goose as he spoke.

His words sent a cold shiver through her and she knew that her father had been trying to shield his family from the reality of the situation. Hester's dreams of contentment as Jonathan's wife fled as she realised why her father wanted her to marry so soon. In normal times she would have been betrothed for several months at least. But the sooner the wedding took place, the sooner she would be safely ensconced in Thomas's country house.

Although she understood her father's reasoning, her heart rebelled and, as she stepped onto London Bridge and hurried towards her home, she scanned the shipping on the river. But there was no sign of the *Caroline*. Surely he must come soon, she thought.

Loving Jonathan as she did, how could she marry old, fat, ugly Thomas, however right he might be? She cared not for her own safety and resolved to enlist her mother's help in delaying her marriage. Elizabeth could truly say that her daughter was needed at home while she was confined to her bed. Mother will understand, she'll make Father realise how impossible it is, Hester thought.

She entered the house and put her basket on the table, turning to Elizabeth, lying on her couch in the corner. Before she could speak, a spasm of pain crossed her mother's face and she saw the thin fingers clutching at the sweat-soaked sheets.

'Mother, what is it?' she cried, kneeling at the sick woman's side.

'Fetch your aunt,' Elizabeth gasped. 'It's too soon, but I think the baby's coming.'

Hester clasped her mother's hand and called frantically for Nellie. The little maid appeared in the doorway, biting her knuckles as she realised what was happening.

'You must go for Mistress Blake or one of the neighbours,' Hester said.

When the girl hesitated Hester spoke with unaccustomed sharpness. 'Either you go, or you stay and tend to my mother. She needs help.'

'I'll go, miss,' Nellie said and hurried out of the house.

By the time Nellie returned, Hester's hand ached where her mother had gripped it each time a pain came. When her aunt came into the room and began to bustle about, taking charge of the situation with her usual brisk efficiency, Hester moved away from the bed and stood, watching helplessly.

'Don't just stand there, girl. Heat some water and tear up those old sheets. We may have need of them before the night is done,' Mary ordered, and Hester hastened to obey, glad to be doing something useful.

Young as she was, she knew the dangers of childbirth. Only last year she'd seen her mother in similar straits. Hours of agony she'd endured, only to give birth to a tiny wizened creature that never even drew its first breath. 'Should we fetch my father?' she asked.

'Men are no use in situations like this,' Mary replied with a grim laugh. 'Time enough when the child is here.'

She turned to shield Hester's gaze from the worst of what was happening. But she could not shut her ears to the sounds of distress coming from the corner of the room. Nellie retreated to the kitchen, leaving her to assist her aunt as best she could.

★ ★ ★

At last, after what seemed like hours, Elizabeth gave a huge sigh. There was a small silence, followed by the pitiful mewling of the new baby.

Mary turned to Hester in triumph. 'You have a little brother. Now it's time to fetch your father. He'll want to see his son.'

Hester's eyes filled with tears. A brother. After all these years of trying, Elizabeth had given Charles a son. Murmuring a silent prayer of thanks, she ran out of the house and along the street towards Cheapside.

Charles was just finishing off a pair of boots. Giving hurried instructions to the journeymen and apprentices, he followed Hester back to the house. Kneeling at his wife's side, he kissed her and the baby, then clasped his hands in a prayer of thanks for the safe delivery of a son.

By the time Dan and Will came home, all signs of the birth had been cleared away and Nellie had recovered her spirits sufficiently to prepare a simple meal. The boys entered apprehensively, but their trepidation swiftly turned to beaming smiles when Nellie greeted them. 'Master Wright has a son, thanks be to God.'

Mary put a hand on Nellie's arm, saying, 'Hush, girl. The mistress is worn out. Let her rest.' She shooed the young people through to the kitchen. 'We will eat in here tonight.'

Hester could not eat. She was thankful that her mother's ordeal was over and that Charles was happy with his son. But she had noted the shadows beneath Elizabeth's eyes, her shallow breathing and heightened colour. She carried a tankard of ale to where her father sat, his eyes anxiously on his wife. The baby stirred in his wooden crib beside the bed and let out a thin wail. Elizabeth started up and reached for the child.

Hester lifted him from the crib and placed him in her mother's arms. As she stood gazing down at the wizened little creature that was her longed-for brother, Mary appeared at her side. 'You'd best go to bed, child,' she said. 'It has been a long day and we'll be busy enough tomorrow with a little one to see to. Your mother is very weak, and likely to remain so for a while. She'll be looking to us to keep the household running smoothly.'

Mary spoke truly and Hester, although

still anxious at Jonathan's continued absence, nursed her mother and baby James devotedly. The baby was still weak and would not suck. Even had he been stronger, Elizabeth had very little milk. But she tried to feed him, reluctant to engage a wet-nurse for fear of bringing the plague to the house.

In despair, Mary devised a method of feeding James by soaking a cloth in milk and getting him to suck on it. Each morning one of the apprentices would go for milk from the dairy which stood at the Southwark end of the bridge before going on to Cheapside to his work.

Hester and Nellie took turns in feeding the child, a task requiring much time and patience. It was a thankless task, too, for it was hard to decide whether he had taken sufficient nourishment.

As the intense heat continued, both mother and child became weaker. Hester began to dread the mewling cry of her little brother. It distressed her that she could do nothing for him.

With the household revolving around the mistress and the new baby, Hester was too busy to dwell on her father's decision to marry her off to Thomas Latham. But the date agreed for the wedding, her eighteenth birthday at the beginning of September, was fast approaching and still Jonathan had not come home.

When he returns, he will speak to my father. Once he knows we wish to wed, surely he will see that I cannot marry Master Latham, Hester thought. But she knew she hoped in vain. Girls of her station in life did what their parents wished. And Hester was a dutiful daughter. She knew that Charles' business was not doing well. His mind would be easier if he knew his beloved daughter would be well provided for.

It was hard to push Thomas Latham to the back of her mind. She had hoped that he would remain in the country as more cases of the plague appeared each day. But his business had brought him back to the city and he was often at the house these days. He would suddenly appear when she was engrossed in her household tasks, pulling her against him and breathing insinuating whispers into her ear.

He had crept up behind her now, clasping her round the waist. His touch made her shiver and the thought of being his wife and having to endure those hot hands on her whenever he wished, made her feel sick. How will I bear it, she thought, desperately trying to twist away from him.

'Come, my pretty. Surely you're not shy? After all, we are to be wed within a few weeks. A little kiss for your betrothed?' Thomas was smiling but his hands gripped her like a vice.

'Master Latham, please let me go. I must go to my brother.' The baby's weak cry came from the cradle which was now set in the corner of the kitchen so that he did not disturb his mother.

'Let the maid see to it,' Thomas said carelessly. 'I must go downriver on business on the morrow and will not be back until a few days before the wedding.'

Even as she struggled, Hester's heart leapt. Maybe Jonathan would be back before Master Latham returned. Wild thoughts of running away with her lover swept through her head, only to be dashed as Thomas pulled her roughly towards him and fastened his lips on her neck. 'Come, my love — a farewell kiss from my bride.' He pinched her cheek and smiled. 'In a short while, my dear, you will be in no position to deny me.'

She kicked his shin and he let go of her abruptly. His little eyes narrowed in anger and Hester shrunk away from him. Then to her consternation, he started to laugh. 'It seems I've picked a wildcat for my bride,' he said. 'Well, I look forward to taming her.'

He pushed her away, picked up his plumed hat and swaggered to the door as Nellie came in and went to the cradle where baby James was now sobbing.

'I'll leave you to your duties, Mistress Hester. But I'll be back for our wedding.'

3

Hester went to the window, hoping that Nellie hadn't noticed her distress. But the maid was engrossed in the baby.

'Poor mite. He came too soon,' she said. It was hot in the kitchen and Nellie wiped a hand across her forehead, pushing back the strands of hair that had fallen from beneath her mobcap. 'And poor Master Wright. He seems torn between pleasure at the birth of a son, and fear for his wife. Do you think the mistress will be all right?'

Hester hastened to reassure the girl, although her own heart was heavy. Each successive pregnancy had left her mother weaker and she feared her recovery would take many months. She knew that, even if the baby did not live, there would be no more attempts at providing Charles with a son.

But the baby would survive, she told

herself. Mary had gone to look for a wet nurse, despite their fears of the plague. If nothing was done the child would die. Hester prayed she would find a strong woman to care for little James and that soon he would begin to grow fat and strong.

The door opened and Mary came in, her face flushed from the heat, despair in her eyes. She was alone. 'No-one is willing to come,' she said in answer to Hester's inquiry.

She lowered her voice, glancing at Elizabeth. 'I have tramped all over Southwark and even farther afield. There are some cases of plague there too. But even so, they fear coming into the city. I found one woman who had just lost her child and had milk aplenty. But when I told them where we lived, her husband refused to allow her to come.'

'What will we do, Aunt?'

'Just keep trying, but if I am unsuccessful, then all we can do is pray.'

Hester had done nothing but pray since her mother's labour had started and privately doubted that it would help. But being a well brought up Christian girl, she smiled and agreed.

Mary's search for a wet nurse continued unsuccessfully and, as the unseasonal heat continued, both Elizabeth and the baby declined. Hester and her aunt did not give up hope however, and each morning one or other of them would leave the house early to fetch fresh milk from the dairy at the southern end of London Bridge.

Then each of them would take turns in coaxing little James to suck some nourishment from a clean rag dipped in the milk. It did him little good, however. The cow's milk was too rich for his weak system and more often than not he brought most of it up again.

Still Hester persevered, spending many hours devotedly tending the baby. But she began to dread the weak mewling cry of her little brother. It distressed her that, despite all her efforts, it seemed she could do nothing for him.

The household revolved around the mistress and the new baby and Hester kept herself busy, trying not to dwell on her father's decision to marry her off to Thomas Latham. Her seventeenth birthday, the date agreed for the wedding, was fast approaching and if her mother regained her strength, it would go ahead as planned.

'Jonathan, where are you? Why do you not return?' she whispered to herself in the long nights when the enduring heat kept her sleepless. Surely he would speak to her father. Once he knows we wish to wed, surely he will see that I cannot marry Master Latham, she thought. But she knew she hoped in vain.

If only she could bring herself to tell him how disrespectfully he treated her when no-one else was there. But Charles was blind to everything but the man's wealth and standing in the city.

Behind her, Nellie was doing her best to soothe the fretful baby. Despite the increase in the number of plague victims over the past few weeks, the little maid seemed to have overcome her fears, although she seldom left the house, spending much of her time with the sickly child. Caring for him had given her something to worry about besides herself.

Hester's thoughts grew bitter, as she reflected on the rapid spread of infection through the city. So many people dying. But Master Latham could come and go as he pleased without hurt. Why could he not die? 'Oh please God, let him die of the plague,' she murmured.

No sooner had the words been formed than Hester gave a gasp of horror. 'Oh Lord, please forgive me for my wicked thoughts,' she whispered.

To make amends, she was especially attentive to her mother for the rest of the evening to the extent that Charles remarked to his wife, 'How blessed we are to have such a dutiful daughter.'

Hester felt another pang of guilt. But the thought once planted in her head would not go away. The death tolls were mounting. Why should Master Latham not be one of the afflicted?

★ ★ ★

The *Caroline* had been on her way home from Spain bringing a fine cargo of leather, silver and other goods when she was attacked by a Dutch privateer. They had managed to avoid capture, but the Captain had been injured. After only a few short months as mate, Jonathan found himself in charge of the ship.

Evading the enemy frigate had called on all his skills, but they had managed to make port at Falmouth on the Cornish coast. There, Jonathan assessed the damage and decided it was not safe to proceed up the Channel. They must do some makeshift repairs before making for home.

Reporting to Captain Ingram who was strapped in his hammock to support his broken leg, Jonathan said, 'I fear it may take some time. I have made inquiries and the timber we require is not available.'

'You have ordered it though, Blake?'

'Of course, Sir. A few days at most.'

Jonathan made arrangements for Captain Ingram to stay at a quayside inn, close to where the *Caroline* was moored. There he could rest his injured leg while keeping an eye on the repairs.

Progress was slow and Jonathan tried to hide his impatience. The men worked hard enough and it was not their fault that the timber was not available. He told himself that Hester would understand. She knew it was a sailor's lot to be far from home for much of the time. But she loved him and would wait for him. As he toiled alongside his men in the searing heat of that mid-summer, he pictured her lovely face and knew that the joy of their reunion would be all the sweeter for the delay.

When he realised it would be yet another week before they could even think of getting under sail, he sent a messenger to the ship owner explaining what had happened and reassuring him that his cargo was safe. He also enclosed a note to Hester, begging his master to get one of his clerks to deliver it to the house on London Bridge.

He did not expect an answer. It would take days for the messenger to reach London and they would probably be under way before he finally docked at Wapping.

At last the repairs were finished and Jonathan took his leave of Captain Ingram, who was to remain in Falmouth until his leg had healed.

'I hope you are in better health when next we meet, Sir,' Jonathan said, shaking the captain's hand.

'It will not be on board the *Caroline*, I fear.' Captain Ingram shifted on his couch and grimaced with pain. 'I think

I will not command a ship again, even if this leg of mine heals well — which I doubt.' He sighed. 'Well, young Blake, my loss is your gain. You have worked well under my command, and if you get the ship safely back to London, I am sure your reward will be a command of your own. I shall certainly recommend this to the owner.'

'Thank you, Sir. I am grateful for your confidence in me.' Jonathan wished he felt the same confidence. Despite a recent victory in a naval engagement with the Dutch, England was still at war and the risk to shipping in the Channel was still great.

Captain Ingram smiled reassuringly and returned Jonathan's firm handshake. 'Farewell, Master Blake. When next we met I will surely address you as Captain Blake.'

The flush of pleasure remained as Jonathan left the inn and hurried across the quayside. Before he mounted the gangplank he turned and saw that Captain Ingram watched from the window. He raised his hand, sorrow for the man's plight mingling with pride as he stepped on board and began issuing orders for their departure.

As the ship began to move away from the quay into the deep water channel, another smaller ship hove to alongside them. As always when two ships came close enough to exchange greetings, the men shouted across the news.

The *Nancy King* had come from London and the reports they passed on brought a chill to Jonathan's heart.

'Are you sure 'tis the plague?' he asked.

'No doubt of it,' the captain of the *Nancy King* said. 'If you are making for London, I fear you will get no further than Gravesend. The city is closed to all newcomers and the authorities will deal harshly with any who try to slip through.'

Before the ships parted company, Jonathan learned how severe the epidemic was — far worse than in previous years. The Mayor of London and the magistrates had instigated the forty day quarantine on all houses affected by the disease — a practice that had been set up more than thirty years before when the last great infection had swept the city. It had rarely been enforced until now.

The news was a terrible blow to Jonathan — his whole world was bound up in the house on London Bridge. He prayed for his mother and Hester and her family. It was all he could do — that and pile on all the sail he dared to get the ship through the Channel and up to the Thames Estuary. Worrying about his loved ones could lead to disaster though. He needed to concentrate on using all his seaman's skills to get the ship home.

When he reached Gravesend, he would make his report to Master Phillips, then hasten upstream to the city. No mayor or magistrate, day or night watchman would keep him from his beloved.

4

The plague began to spread more rapidly and Hester was glad of the excuse to stay at home and help Nellie with nursing her mother and caring for baby James. She found a kind of contentment in looking after her little brother, and with the knowledge that Master Latham had left the city for a few days, she became almost light-hearted.

There had been talk of closing the city gates against incomers and she hoped it would happen before he returned. It would be a relief to be spared his attentions.

Aunt Mary still kept up her visits to the sick and needy and did the marketing on her way home each day. She seemed unconcerned by the threat of infection, although she never hugged or kissed Hester as she used to, and she had never held the baby in her arms.

'If we are sensible, there is no reason for us to be afflicted,' she said, when Hester urged her to take more care. 'I am convinced that it is the overcrowding and filth that the poor people have to endure that makes them so susceptible. I counsel them to trust in God and to keep themselves clean and all will be well.' She sighed. 'Though the latter seems an impossibility, given the conditions they live in.'

It was another day of blistering heat and Hester was weary of trying to get the baby to suck on the milk-soaked cloth she held to his mouth. The river beyond the window looked cool and inviting and Hester thought longingly of her childhood when she and Jonathan and the apprentices would take off their shoes and stockings and paddle at the edge of the water. Such pleasures were forbidden her now that she was grown and soon to marry.

She frowned, thinking of the wedding which was not far off now. She had resigned herself to becoming Thomas's wife, managing to convince herself that if Jonathan truly cared he would have found a way to let her know why he had not returned at the appointed time.

Each morning at family worship, Charles prayed for his safe return but Hester knew that his mother had almost given up hope. If his ship had been wrecked or seized by privateers it might be many months before they knew what had happened. Meantime, Hester would become Mistress Latham and must school herself not to dream of Jonathan. But the small spark of hope could not be extinguished and would not be until Thomas had placed the ring upon her finger.

When Mary came home, Hester looked up eagerly, hopeful for news as she always was. But a frown creased her aunt's homely features as she set her basket down on the table. She sat at the table, wiping her forehead with the corner of her shawl.

'Are you all right, Aunt?' Hester

asked in concern.

'Don't worry about me, child. It's just this never-ending heat.' Mary sighed. 'I've just heard that the south end of the bridge is to be closed and nobody will be allowed in or out of the city. They're trying to stop the sickness from spreading.'

Despite her earlier thoughts, the news now filled Hester with fear. If the city was closed, what hope was there for those left behind? The King and the court had already moved to Oxford and those rich enough had fled to the country. And what of Jonathan?

Mary echoed her thoughts. 'My poor son. Even if he is still alive and tries to come home, they won't let him through the gates. But at least if his ship is safe, he will be too. No shipping is to be allowed up the Thames until the distemper has run its course.'

Hester choked back a sob. What was to become of them? Her thoughts were interrupted by James' cries and she called Nellie to bring a fresh bowl of warm milk. Once more, she dipped the rag in it and tried to coax James to suck some nourishment from it. But he was too weak and his pitiful cries grew louder.

Cradling him in her arms, Hester paced up and down the room, trying to get him to settle, afraid that his cries would distress her mother. But her mother's faint voice called, 'Give him to me, daughter.' Hester put the baby in Elizabeth's arms, smiling at the look of content on her face, even as James continued to cry weakly.

She walked to the window and looked out at the sparkling river. There were fewer ships than usual. The laden merchant vessels that usually thronged the wharves had been avoiding the stricken city for some weeks, unloading their precious cargoes at some other port where others would reap the benefit. From today, there would be no ships at all.

Everyone suffered during the time of plague, Hester thought. No wonder her father was so worried. The gentry for whom he fashioned such high-quality leather goods had fled to the country, many of them without paying their bills. And as if the plague were not enough, the continuing war with Holland had affected trade also.

Worrying about her father brought her thoughts to Thomas Latham again and she felt a little lift of her spirits. He had not returned from his trip down-river and, now that the city gates were closed, she would be spared his odious attentions for a while longer. Maybe the wedding would be postponed, she thought smiling, even as she shuddered at the thought of becoming his wife.

So engrossed was she in her thoughts that she scarcely noticed the deathly hush in the room behind her. For once, her baby brother wasn't crying. But before she could feel any relief that he was sleeping at last, the quiet room was rent with a terrible cry. Her mother's shrieks pierced the air. 'Oh, God, please, how could you do this to me?

My baby, oh my baby.'

Hester hastened to Elizabeth's side and gently tried to take James from her, calling frantically for Mary. But despite her weakness, Elizabeth hung on to the pitiful bundle, clutching him to her breast.

'Mother, please. Let me see if I can help him,' Hester begged.

'You can do nothing. He's dead. God has taken him from me, just as he did the others.' Elizabeth began to sob quietly.

Mary came into the room and gently pushed Hester out of the way. 'You must fetch your father,' she said.

'Oh, please, no. Do not make me be the one to tell him. Let me stay and comfort my mother,' Hester cried.

Mary hesitated. 'Maybe Nellie could go,' she murmured, then shook her head. 'I'll go. I'll fetch the priest as well.' She took her cloak from behind the door and hurried out.

Elizabeth still clutched the child, rocking to and fro as tears streamed down her cheeks. Hester didn't know what to do. Swallowing the lump in her throat, she went through to the kitchen where Nellie cowered, hands over her ears to shut out the dreadful cries from the other room.

She turned a pale frightened face as Hester entered the room. 'Oh, mistress, what has happened? Is it the plague?'

'No, Nellie. It's little James. He's dead.'

The maid's eyes filled with tears but Hester gave her no time to dwell on what had happened. 'Mistress Blake has gone to the workshop to fetch my father. Will you heat some water so that I can wash the child? Hurry now.'

While she waited for her father, Hester sat beside her mother, who still rocked the child in her arms. Gradually her sobs eased and her breathing became laboured. As if the death of her longed-for son had given her a reason to struggle no more, Elizabeth was slipping deeper into a world where none could reach her. Yet still she clutched the baby to her bosom, unwilling to relinquish the tiny bundle, even to Hester. By the time Charles stumbled breathlessly into the house, Elizabeth had breathed her last.

Hester had never heard a man cry before and, as her father's wrenching sobs filled the room, she fled to her own bed-chamber. There she paced up and down. 'It's my wickedness that has brought this upon us,' she muttered. 'God has punished me for wishing Master Latham dead.'

She went to the window, but even the sight of her beloved River Thames could not bring her solace now. Her thoughts turned to Jonathan, then quickly away. She would not remember his laughing blue eyes. She must make amends and be the dutiful daughter her father wanted. She would marry Master Latham.

5

Hester could not rid herself of her guilty feelings. She truly felt she was being punished for her wicked thoughts. Her guilt increased when her mother and the baby were not allowed a proper burial. The news of two deaths at the home of Master Wright spread rapidly along the bridge and the watchmen arrived at the house just as Mary returned with the Reverend Taylor, Rector of St Giles. It had taken her a while to find him for his services were in great demand at this terrible time.

She did not enter the house. Standing at the door, she spoke quietly to Hester. 'The watch will close up the house now. If I remain outside, I will be in a better position to help you all. I will stay with friends in the city and call here each day to see how you fare.'

'But, Aunt, we do not have the

plague here,' Hester protested.

'The fear of contagion is so great that none will believe it,' Mary said.

'That is true,' the Reverend Taylor said. Nevertheless, he stepped over the threshold and offered his condolences to the family, apologising for the fact that he held a handkerchief to his face while he spoke the prayers.

'I would not wish to bring the infection to you, if what you say is true,' he said. 'And I must think of my parishioners. I cannot risk carrying the infection to them when I leave here.' He finished the prayers and went on his way after telling them that the officers of the watch would be there at nightfall to take the bodies away.

Charles' protests went unheeded and when the men arrived, he retreated to his chamber upstairs, unable to bear the thought of his wife and child sharing a common burial ground with victims of the plague.

The watchman, the same man who had informed Hester of the closure of the bridge, spoke gruffly. 'I have my orders, Mistress,' he said. 'We can take no chances while the plague is spreading so quickly.'

Hester tried to smile. He was trying to be kind, but he had probably seen so much grief in the past few weeks, it was hard for him to show sympathy. She watched dry-eyed, unable even to pray, as the bodies of her mother and baby brother were moved from the house and placed on the cart with others. Hester averted her eyes, but not before she had seen that little James was not the only child. Then the tears did come.

The watchman stood guard as a large red cross was painted on the front door and boards nailed across it. Before the house was sealed, Charles asked Mary to go to the workshop. 'See how the lads fare and tell them they will have to stay there until we are allowed out again,' he said. 'Assure them that I trust them to do what they can to keep things safe.'

Tears rolled down Mary's cheeks.

'You can depend on me, Charles. And I will come each day or send Dan or Will with provisions. Don't worry about me. I will stay with friends.'

At least they would not lack for food and water, Hester thought with relief as she leaned from the window to bid her aunt a fond farewell. Then the watchman sealed it with planks nailed roughly into place.

Nellie began to wail as darkness fell in the room and Hester hastened to comfort her. 'At least we have someone to fetch food and water until the epidemic is over. My aunt will look after us,' she said, leading the girl through to the kitchen overlooking the river. 'See how lucky we are, Nellie,' she said. 'We do not have to spend our days in darkness or candlelight, like those who live within the city. We can leave our window open to the air and watch the comings and goings on the river. It is less of a prison than some poor souls have to endure.'

Nellie sniffed and dried her eyes. 'Are

you sure we should leave the window open? Will not the bad air bring the fever to us?'

'I am sure that is not so. No-one knows how the disease travels. And I for one would rather die breathing God's fresh air, than be stifled in this heat,' Hester declared.

At the mention of dying, Nellie once more burst into tears and Hester managed to assuage her own grief in trying to comfort the girl. At last she made her way up to bed, hoping that sleep would bring some sort of relief from the ordeals of the day. But she lay wakeful long into the night and at last left her bed to sit by the window, where a faint breeze cooled her fevered thoughts. Her last comforting thought before she finally fell asleep in the chair was that, with the house boarded up, Master Latham would have to stay away. And there would be no wedding — for a while at least.

Lost in her own grief, Hester was unable to comfort her father, who'd scarcely touched food or drink for days.

Nellie too was beyond comfort, weeping copious tears into her apron.

At last, Hester lost patience. 'We are all grieving, Nellie,' she snapped. 'Now, we must care for the living. Go to the window and see if Dan has arrived with meat and ale.'

Nellie wiped her face with her apron. Her face was blotched with tears but she summoned a smile at the thought of seeing Dan. The boys had taken it in turn to row a small boat from the riverbank to the house in the middle of the bridge. Fortunately, the windows giving on to the river had not been sealed and Nellie had made it her task to lower a basket containing a few coins soaked in vinegar to pay for their provisions. Dan or Will would place the bread and ale, and meat if it was available, into the basket and she would haul it into the kitchen.

It was a chance for Nellie to exchange a few words with the young lad she had fallen in love with, and Hester sometimes envied her. She had almost given up hope of ever seeing Jonathan again.

Mary came each day and spoke to them through a crack in the boards across the windows at the front of the house. And each day Hester asked, with hope fading from her voice, if there was any news.

At least there was no sign of Thomas Latham. Hester hoped he had still been out of town when the city gates were barred. She still felt guilty for wishing him dead but her guilt was somewhat assuaged by the knowledge that he had left the city before it was closed. At least he would be safe. But the thought that her mother's death was somehow a punishment for having such wicked thoughts would not go away. And there was no-one to confide in. Even the priest had not been near the house since that dreadful day.

There was no time to brood, however, as all her efforts were concentrated on trying to lift her father out of his depression. He was drinking large amounts of wine and ale and spent most of each day sunk in his chair beside the empty fireplace. Even the daily family prayers had been abandoned.

Hester was sitting by the riverside window mending a tear in her skirt when Nellie came through from the kitchen. The apprentices had not come today and she was ready to burst into tears again.

'There is plenty of time, Nellie. There are still some hours to sunset. They will come soon,' Hester reassured the younger girl. She was worried, too, but she could not let Nellie see her fear.

The maid managed to smile through her tears. 'I don't know how I would have got through these days without you, Miss,' she said. 'What will I do when you leave us to be married?'

'It will not be for a long while yet,' Hester said and felt a little lift of her heart. No wedding could take place until a year after the death of her mother. Grief for her mother and her fears for Jonathan had pushed the thought of her approaching wedding to the back of her mind. 'Even when the plague had run its course, I cannot marry while we are in mourning,' she told the maid.

The deferment of her fate brought a little relief to Hester and she resolved that for the time remaining with her father, she would be the dutiful daughter he thought her to be. Who knew what could happen in a year?

The next day, as Nellie leaned from the kitchen window awaiting Dan or Will with their provisions, Hester took stock of their small remaining store of flour and salt. If neither of the apprentices appeared today, they would have to start rationing the food they had left. Mary had not been near the house for several days either and Hester prayed that she and the boys were safe.

Her prayers were without conviction though. How could she believe they would be answered when each night they heard the doleful clang of the bell and the cries of the night-watchman calling, 'Bring out your dead'? The rumble of the death wagons along the cobbled streets carried on the night air, along with the grief-stricken wailing of the survivors.

Nellie's excited voice brought Hester into the kitchen. 'The boat's here, Miss. It's Dan.'

'Ask if there's news of Mistress Blake,' she said, pushing past the girl and leaning out of the window. Before she could speak, however, she gave a gasp at the apparition seated in the stern of the boat. A cloaked figure, its face covered with a leather mask with a huge protruding beak, greeted her.

When he spoke, she realised it was Master Latham. So he had not left the city after all. He must have been here all the time and he had not even tried to call and pay his condolences to her father, his supposed friend. Dread of the plague affected them all, but Hester could not hide her scorn for the man, who, even before the epidemic, had been unable to conceal his fear.

He laughed when he saw how his appearance had startled her. 'It is indeed I, Mistress. The physicians say these masks will deter the infection. The nose is stuffed with herbs which will filter out the bad air.'

'I hope it is effective, then, sir,' Hester said politely, reflecting to what lengths people would go in their fear of the plague. The knowledge that he could not enter the house made her bold and she leaned from the window. 'I had thought you had left the city since we have not seen you for so long,' she said.

'I returned the day before they closed the gates,' Thomas replied. He made to remove his plumed hat but the boat rocked and he clutched the side. 'My apologies for not calling on you when I heard of the death of your mother. My business has detained me. I trust you are all well?'

'Yes, but my mother and brother did

not have the plague. My aunt has tried to convince the authorities of that but to no avail.'

'I pray it will not be long before you are allowed to leave the house.' Thomas smiled and licked his lips. 'I merely remind you, Mistress Hester — today was to be our wedding day. I regret that it must be postponed but it will not be long now.'

His words seemed to hide a threat and Hester felt herself flush. 'You forget, sir. We are in mourning. There can be no wedding for a year. Perhaps you would like to speak to my father on the matter?'

'There is no need to disturb Master Wright. I will return on the morrow.' This time he managed to sweep off his hat and bow without upsetting the boat.

Nellie hauled up the basket containing bread and fish and placed it on the kitchen table. 'Dan tells me that Will and Mistress Blake are well, but one of the journeymen did not appear at the workshop this morning.' She crossed herself hastily.

As Dan rowed away, pulling strongly against the tide, Hester and Nellie watched from the window until they reached the shore. Pulling the casement closed, Hester said, 'If Master Latham comes tomorrow, tell him I am too busy to speak to him,' she said.

Nellie's eyes widened. 'But, Miss, he is your betrothed.'

'But not yet my husband,' Hester snapped. 'I owe him no obedience yet.'

Nellie hurriedly began to unpack the provisions whilst Hester returned to her mending. Watching the maid as she worked, Hester was ashamed of her sharpness. 'I am pleased that Dan remains in good health. It will be a happy day when the boys return. We must make a feast for them and my aunt.'

'Please God, it will not be long now, Miss, if what Master Latham says is true,' she replied.

The next morning, when Mary Blake

knocked on the door, Hester almost cried with relief. Although Dan had assured her all was well, she had not quite believed it.

Mary spoke through the closed door. 'Hester dear, do not be distressed. Your long incarceration is almost over. The city fathers say that the number of cases is diminishing. But they will not open the city gates until some days have passed with no new cases being reported.'

'My father will be pleased. He has been fretting about the workshop.'

'I called there myself on the way here,' Mary replied. 'There has been much looting in the city but, thanks to the presence of the apprentices, your father's premises have been spared.'

'What of the journeymen — any news?'

'There can be only one reason why they have not appeared at the workshop. But at least the apprentices seem to remain in good health. They have done well to keep the workshop running smoothly.'

'Thank God,' Hester said, then abruptly, 'Master Latham was here yesterday.'

'I have spoken to him also,' Mary said. 'He bid me tell you that although there can be no wedding yet, he is willing to wait. He thinks very well of you and I'm sure he will make an excellent husband. You will be well set up, the wife of such a wealthy man. And if, God forbid, you should be widowed young like me, you will not be thrown upon the mercy of your relations as I was.'

A cold shiver ran down Hester's spine. She would not be sorry when the restrictions were lifted, but that meant Master Latham would come visiting once more. She wanted to ask if there had been any new of Jonathan or the *Caroline*, but she could not bring herself to speak his name.

Mary seemed to sense her thoughts. 'When the gates are opened, perhaps we shall have news of my son,' she said.

'Even if he had returned, he would not have been allowed into the city.'

'Do not give up hope, Aunt,' Hester said, as much to comfort herself as anything. 'The pestilence is waning. Please God, things will soon return to normal.'

But it was the middle of October before the pestilence began to abate sufficiently to allow travellers into the city. And still no word came of the young man Hester loved. She and Mary grieved anew, convinced he too must have perished in the plague.

6

The plague had reached its worst by the time Jonathan had reached Gravesend some weeks ago. When the *Caroline* docked, he had hurried to the office of the harbour master, hungry for news from the capital. What he heard was worse than anything he had imagined on the journey up the Channel and into the estuary.

Many had fled the city, the death tolls were the highest ever experienced in any previous epidemic. Fear for his loved ones clutched his heart. The *Caroline's* owner, Master Phillips, was fulsome in his praise for his handling of the disaster, as well as bringing the ship safely home, and offered him the captaincy of the vessel. But even the promise of a share of the profits if the next voyage was successful could not cheer him.

When Jonathan refused Master Phillips' offer and declared his intention of seeking news of his family, the man was horrified. There had been a few cases of the plague in Gravesend and even here there was talk of quarantining the port. 'You cannot go, Master Blake,' he declared. 'At least make this one voyage for me. By the time you return the plague will surely have abated and you can visit your family then.'

'I am sorry, Master Phillips. Surely you see that I must go.' Jonathan was adamant, and the following morning he set off on foot for the capital. He had tried without success to find a small boat owner willing to row him upriver, even if only a short way. But no-one dared to brave the water bailiffs who were determined to keep further infection out of the city.

As he journeyed on foot through the Kent countryside, he realised that even the small towns and villages along the way had suffered the pestilence. The continuing sunshine had brought an early ripening of the wheat and the harvest should have been well under way. But everywhere he saw fields half cut, the wheat lying where it fell.

At last he reached the outskirts of the city, trudging wearily through the suburbs of Bermondsey and South-wark. As he approached the south end of London Bridge, he prayed fervently that he would find his loved ones safe.

The roadway on to the bridge was barred and the watchman called to ask his business, careful not to approach too closely. Jonathan wondered at his caution. If things were as bad as he had been led to believe, surely the watch-man was in more danger from the city he guarded than from strangers with-out.

'I seek news of my mother, Mistress Blake, and her cousin, Mistress Wright,' he said.

'I cannot let you pass, young sir. And if you had seen the sights I had these past two months and more, you would not wish to,' the man said.

'But I must find out if they are well,' Jonathan said, despair clutching at his heart. To be almost within sight of his loved one's house and not to see her sweet face was almost more than he could bear.

'I do not know of whom you speak. The names are not familiar to me,' the watchman said. 'I have only been on this post a few days. My predecessor succumbed last week.'

'Please, Sir. Can you not find out for me? Their house is yonder, on the bridge. Just ask for Mister Wright, the leather craftsman. Everybody knows him.' Jonathan pleaded.

'I'm sorry, I cannot leave my post.' He gestured with his pike at the houses crowding the bridge. 'There you see, every house is afflicted, your master's too. All are dead or dying. You can see the red crosses from here.'

Jonathan's shoulders slumped. His journey had been in vain. He turned away, head lowered in despair, not wanting to accept that he would never see his dear sweetheart's face again, nor hear her musical laughter.

Not caring where he went, he started back along the road. A stout merchant barred his path and Jonathan stared into a face he knew.

'Did I hear you asking for the Wrights?' the man asked.

Jonathan had never liked Thomas Latham but today the pleasure of seeing a familiar face overcame his dislike. 'Oh, Master Latham, can you tell me how Master Wright and his family fare,' he cried.

Thomas frowned. 'You have not heard of the tragedy then, Master Blake?'

Jonathan's heart sank. 'Who? My mother, Mistress Hester?' he stammered.

The other man laid a hand on Jonathan's sleeve, his face grave. 'All have succumbed. God rest their souls.'

Jonathan stumbled away, careless of the unmanly tears coursing down his cheeks. Hester, his mother, Master

Wright who had been like a father to him — all victims of the cruel pestilence. How could he bear it? And where would he go now? What would he do?

He did not look back, nor see Master Thomas Latham staring after him, a cruel smile twisting his lips. 'You shall not have her,' he muttered.

* * *

Autumn came, and with it cool breezes and soft showers. Many said that the wind and rain would wash away the pestilence, and it was true that not so many people were dying now and fewer new cases were being reported compared with a few weeks ago.

The King and his court stayed away but many, especially the merchants and tradesmen, began to return to the city, and by the end of the year there was some indication that things were returning to normal.

By the time the quarantine on

London Bridge had been lifted, Hester's father had begun to recover his spirits. Charles still grieved for his wife and son, but Hester was pleased that he was starting to take an interest in things again.

There was plenty for him to do if he wanted to get his business back on its former footing. The three journeymen he employed had died soon after the Wrights had been shut up in their house and the apprentices had been left to carry on as best they could.

'I have to confess, they have made a good job of things and I am well pleased with their efforts,' Charles told Hester on his return from Cheapside on their first day of freedom.

'They will no doubt be pleased you are back, though, to give them guidance in their work,' Hester said, as she helped Nellie set the table for their evening meal.

The lads came in and took their places at the table. After grace had been said and thanks given to God for their safe deliverance from the plague, Charles held up a hand for silence. 'Before we begin I have an announcement to make,' he said.

Hester's hand paused in ladling out the broth and she held her breath. Surely it was too soon to announce her wedding plans. They were still in mourning after all. But at his next words she let out her breath and smiled with genuine pleasure.

'I know that Dan still has a year of his apprenticeship to run, but he has proved his worth and more these past weeks,' Charles said. 'I could not have left my business in better hands.' He leaned across the table and shook the apprentice's hand. 'Henceforth you are no longer a humble apprentice, but a journeyman and my right-hand man.'

'Thank you, Sir.' Dan's flush of pleasure deepened to crimson as Nellie threw down the basket of bread she had just brought from the kitchen and kissed him soundly on the cheek.

'Does that mean we can be wed?' she cried.

'Not so fast, Nellie. It is the man's duty to ask for your hand and he still has to ask for my father's permission.' Hester laughed, knowing that Charles' permission was sure to be given freely. They had all seen the love blossoming between the young couple. Pleased as she was for them, Hester was a little uneasy at the talk of weddings. It would not be long before Thomas Latham came calling again and she would have to face the inescapable.

As winter approached, the nightmare of those plague-ridden summer months gradually faded and the household returned to normal. Although Hester still missed her mother unbearably, she could still take pleasure in seeing Nellie smiling. Charles, too, seemed to have thrown off his depression and went off to his workshop each day with more than a spring in his step than Hester had seen in many a month.

Mary was the one who caused Hester

most concern. She had aged over the past weeks and, although she still went into the city to continue her work among the sick and poor, her steps were slow and head bowed. She did not voice her grief, but Hester knew she had given up hope of ever seeing her son again. If his ship had not been wrecked by the Dutch, then he must surely have succumbed to the plague.

Hester began to accompany Mary on her rounds of the city's hovels once more, desperate to keep busy in order to take her mind off Jonathan's plight and the moment when she would have to face Master Latham again.

He had sent a message expressing his pleasure that they were no longer in quarantine and promising to visit on his return from Gravesend. Hester shuddered at the thought although she had almost resigned herself to the prospect of marriage. She was beginning to accept that if Jonathan were all right he would surely have returned to London by now.

In addition to helping Mary with her charitable works, Hester took over the running of the household and found some measure of content in looking after her father. Charles was more subdued than he had been before the loss of his wife and baby son, but occasionally his hearty laugh would ring out, and Hester would smile, pleased that he was beginning to regain his zest for life.

Christmas however, was a quiet time for the Wrights. As usual they attended the service at St Giles' Church, which this year was packed as people flocked to give thanks for their deliverance from the plague. It was a solemn group that made their way through the streets to the house on London Bridge, and Hester could not help comparing it with previous years.

Then the house had rung with laughter at the apprentice boys' pranks, and Elizabeth had presided over a table groaning with delicacies. This year, the fare was plentiful but plain and the laughter was tinged with sorrow and a measure of guilt that they had survived when so many others had perished.

On Boxing Day, Hester and Mary filled baskets with leftover food and made their rounds of the hovels of Cheapside. They did not speak much as they hurried along the narrow cobbled alleyways and courts, each of them remembering last year when Jonathan had been with them.

Mary, suspecting how it was between them, had lingered, allowing them to walk ahead and enjoy a few precious moments together. Hester bit back a sob, recalling his tender words and the promise that when he returned from his next voyage, he would ask her father for permission to court her. If only she had known what was in her father's mind, she would have begged Jonathan to speak then. If only he had returned last summer. If only Thomas Latham had died in the plague . . .

She shook her head, regretting her wicked thoughts yet unable to stop them. Mary took her arm and gave it a comforting squeeze. 'I know what you are thinking. I miss him, too,' she said.

Hester bit her lip. She could not confess to her beloved aunt what was in her heart. She must pray for forgiveness and seek redemption in being the dutiful daughter her father thought her to be.

When they reached home, Charles was sitting by the fire and he rose to welcome them. His visitor rose from the chair opposite and Hester caught her breath. Truly she was being punished for her wicked thoughts of just a few moments ago.

'Mistress Blake and Mistress Hester. How delightful to see you both again after so long.' He greeted both of them but his eyes were on Hester and she shrank from his gaze. He gave a sweeping bow in the manner of the court, took her hand and kissed it.

His powdered face with a black patch on his cheek, contrasted strangely with the jet black of his flowing wig. In his blue silk suit and yellow breeches he looked like a strutting peacock and Hester tried to hide her disgust. Did he think that dressing up like one of the aristocracy made him appear more important?

She resisted the urge to snatch her hand away and answered him coolly. 'You are welcome, Master Latham, as are all my father's friends. Has Nellie offered you some refreshment?'

She walked towards the kitchen to call the maid and when she turned he was close behind her.

'I hope my welcome to this house is not just as a friend of your father's, Mistress,' he said quietly.

She did not answer but took the tray of food and drink from Nellie and put it on the table. Busying herself with serving the mulled wine and sweet-meats, she did not at first take in what was being said.

Thomas was telling her father about his trip downriver and the problems he had found in his warehouses at

Gravesend, when Mary interrupted.

'Did you hear aught of the *Caroline* while you were there?' she asked.

Thomas leaned back, a finger to his fleshy lips and appeared lost in thought. 'The *Caroline* — that was the ship your son sailed in was it not, Mistress Blake?'

Mary nodded eagerly. 'What news?'

Thomas shook his head and she gasped. 'I spoke with her owner, Master Phillips. It appears that she was attacked in the Channel — some time last year I believe. The loss of his ship was a severe blow, I fear.'

Mary swayed and put a hand to her lips. 'My son. What of Jonathan?' she whispered.

Hester hastened to her aunt's side and helped her into a chair, holding a glass of wine to her lips. Only she saw the cruel smile that crossed Thomas Latham's face.

'The ship was lost with all hands, so I was led to believe,' he said, bowing over Mary's hand. 'My condolences, Madam.'

97

He returned to his seat by the fire and addressed Charles. 'These are troubling times we live in, Master Wright. I myself have lost several ships to those knavish Dutch pirates.' He muttered a curse under his breath and Hester winced at the profanity.

The men were discussing the war. 'The King cares nothing for affairs of state. He stays at Hampton Court cavorting with his mistresses, while the Dutch play havoc with our shipping in the Channel,' Thomas said.

'They say the plague was visited upon us as a punishment for the wickedness of the Court. But the events of the past year do not seem to have caused the King to mend his ways,' Charles declared. 'I fear it will take more than a brush with the plague to bring him to a sense of his duty.'

Thomas laughed. 'I did not take you for one of these simpletons that look upon the pestilence as a punishment from God.'

'It seems as good an explanation as

any,' Charles said.

Thomas swigged from his tankard and belched. 'Nonsense, my friend. If the King was to be punished, why was he not struck down also? Besides, ever since the return of the King, the Court has been a byword for lechery and depravity.'

'I pray you do not speak of such things in front of the women,' Charles protested. 'Still, what you say is true.'

Hester wanted to join in the conversation, to say that there were worse punishments for wickedness than death. But she did not want to draw Thomas' attention to herself more than necessary. She was already conscious of his eyes on her, raking her body with an insolent gaze.

Hot shame flooded through her as she read the thoughts in his mind.

How could she bear it? But she knew she must endure God's punishment for her wicked thoughts.

★   ★   ★

In the coming months Thomas was often at the house on London Bridge. Hester tried to avoid him by keeping busy in the kitchen, but he seemed to have the gift of knowing when she would be alone. Her skin crawled when he took her hand and kissed it, murmuring as he did so, 'Not long now, my pretty.'

She could not speak to her father about such things, but she longed to confide in Mary. But her aunt had troubles of her own. Despite Master Latham's words, she still could not quite believe that her son had perished, and had taken to haunting the quays and wharves, asking every merchant and seaman for news of Jonathan.

7

The more Hester saw of Thomas during that spring and summer of 1666, the harder it became for her to keep her vow. Many times she was on the point of telling her father she could not go through with the marriage. She even thought of running away, though she had no idea of where she would go.

But then Charles would offer a word of praise for her devotion to her family, commend her as a dutiful daughter, and she knew she would never shame him by attempting to break her betrothal. As the weeks passed, the feeling that she must atone for her wicked thoughts about Thomas gradually faded.

Surely losing her mother and the man she loved was punishment enough. The thoughts churned in her head as she sat with Mary sewing the new clothes that would befit her status as Mistress Latham, wife of a rich merchant. But she could see no way out of her dilemma.

The summer passed all too quickly for Hester and preparations for her wedding in early September were almost complete. Charles had declared that she must have new gowns and petticoats to take to her husband and he had bought a large quantity of woollens and silks from a merchant friend. Hester could take no pleasure in her new finery, even in the gown of finest pale blue silk which Mary was making for her wedding day.

Hester knew that her father could ill afford such an expense for, despite his assurance that business would pick up once the effects of the plague year had begun to diminish, it had not happened as he'd hoped. Many of his customers had died still owing him money. And, although some of his wealthier patrons had returned to the city, ordering new boots seemed far from their minds.

The plague had left its mark on them all. Almost everyone they knew had lost family or friends to the pestilence. Even those who had not, suffered financially, for in many parts of the country the harvest had been left to rot, and pigs and cows had been slaughtered where there were none left to care for them. The result was that the price of food had soared, especially in the city, and many among the poor were near starvation. Who cared for new boots and shoes when hunger gnawed at the belly?

Charles returned home from the workshop one day, his shoulders bowed, his face careworn. When Hester greeted him with a smile and a kiss on his cheek, his tired eyes lit up and he pulled a package from behind his back.

'A gift for you,' he said, 'the dearest daughter a man has ever been blessed with.'

Hester opened the package to reveal a pair of boots exquisitely worked in the softest calfskin. 'Thank you, Father.'

She kissed him again and fingered the soft leather. 'I don't deserve such a beautiful gift.'

'They are for you to wear on your wedding day,' Charles said. 'You will surely be the most beautiful bride ever to have walked the aisle of St Giles' Church — and no father could be more proud.'

Hester hugged him but her spirits drooped. She thanked the Lord that her father could not see what was in her heart. His words conjured up an image she had been trying to avoid. She almost blurted it out then — that she could not, would not, marry Thomas Latham, even if it meant living in poverty and remaining a spinster all her days.

Before she could speak, however, her father put his hands on her shoulders and his expression was grave. 'I cannot tell you, dear daughter, how pleased I am that soon you will be wed — relieved too. It eases the pain of what I have to tell you now, knowing that you will be provided for in the future.'

Hester grasped his hand. 'Father, what is it?'

Charles shook his head. 'It shames me to tell you, but you will have to know eventually. I am in debt, Hester, and before long the bailiffs will come and take away my goods from the workshop.'

'I knew that times were hard, Father. But how has it come to this?' Hester shook her head, trying to take in what he had just told her.

He sank into a chair and covered his face with his hands. 'It is hard to tell you, my dear. I have been foolish, speculated unwisely as you know. Master Latham lent me money to clear the debt, but I used it to invest more heavily. I had hoped that when my business picked up . . . ' His voice trailed away.

'Surely Master Latham . . . ' It hurt to have to say it, but she had to offer her father what comfort she could. 'He will be your son-in-law before long. He would not wish to see a relative impoverished.'

'You speak truly, daughter. And Master Latham had shown himself to be a honourable man. On your wedding day, my debt to him will be wiped clean.' He sighed. 'But I will still owe money to the suppliers of leather and for the rent on my workshop.'

'Will your creditors not wait for better times? They must know you are a man of honour, well respected in the city. They will get their money eventually.'

'Alas, so many are in the same position as myself. If my creditors had paid me, I would not be in these straits. I would not wish it on another through any fault of mine.'

Hester did not know what else to say. At that moment, seeing her father's distress, she felt that even marriage to Thomas Latham would be bearable if it would help him. She began to see that her foolish thoughts of running away had been merely selfish. Most women married for reasons other than love. Why had she thought things would be different for her?

As the wife of a rich man she would be able to help them all. Her father and Mary would always have a home with her, and Nellie could accompany her to her new home as her maid until she and Dan married. Freed from his indentures, Dan would soon find employment for the skills he had learned from her father and surely Thomas would find work for young Will.

She could not help being vexed however, for she felt that her father had brought too much of his trouble on himself — and upon his family. She began to realise that he had seen her marriage to Thomas Latham as a way out of his difficulty, with no thought of his daughter's happiness.

She could not restrain herself from speaking sharply to him. 'Why then, Father, when you knew times were hard, did you insist on such a show of finery for me? You know I am content with simple gowns and have no need of fine skills and satins. The money could have gone towards payment of your debt.'

'It is natural for a man to want the best for his daughter,' Charles said and he looked so stricken that Hester's soft heart melted. He loved her and had done what he thought best. Besides, it was too late now.

When Thomas called that evening, Hester put herself out to be agreeable to him, refilling his tankard and pulling her chair closer to his before taking up her needlework.

Charles had returned to the workshop and Mary was at the home of a neighbour. Normally Hester would have done anything to avoid being alone with her betrothed. She consoled herself with the thought that Nellie and Dan were in the kitchen and would come quickly if she called.

Thomas took a long draught from his tankard and leaned back in his chair.

His hand reached out and touched Hester's hair. 'You are very quiet this evening, my dear,' he said. 'Your modesty becomes you indeed.' His eyes narrowed and a lascivious smile played over his lips. 'Still, it will not be long before there will be no need for modesty.'

He chuckled and his fingers played with her hair. She steeled herself not to recoil from his touch and looked up at him demurely. 'My father has told me of your kindness, Sir,' she said. 'I thank you.'

'It is a small thing to do for one whom I shall soon be pleased to call father-in-law,' Thomas said with a careless wave of his hand. 'Besides, it pleases me to please you.'

His flowery words should have melted her heart but she could not respond to him. It was not that she had already given her heart to Jonathan. Hester had always felt that there was something behind what Master Latham said, that he meant something other than his most innocent-sounding words.

Now, the expression in his eyes as he leaned towards her, almost caused her to shrink away from him. But she took a deep breath and said, 'I have been thinking, Sir, of the great change it will bring to my life when I become your wife. It will be very strange for me, having charge of so large a household after caring for only my father these past months.'

'Do not concern yourself. Your mother taught you well, my dear. Besides, my servants have been with me this long while and are used to my ways. My housekeeper will inform you of how I like things done.' He took her hand and began fondling her fingers, lowering his voice and glancing towards the door as if to be sure they were alone. 'If that is the true extent of your concern, my dear, you may rest easy. It is not for your housekeeping skills that I asked for your hand in marriage.'

Hester gasped and pulled her hand away. Thomas narrowed his eyes, then burst into throaty laughter. 'How I love to see your chuckle flush in so maidenly a fashion,' he said.

She picked up her needlework again and sewed industriously for a few moments until she was calm again. She had hoped to introduce the subject of her maid gradually. But just when she had steeled herself to ask if Nellie could join the household, he had disconcerted her with his lewd insinuations. There was nothing for it, she would have to ask directly.

Taking a deep breath, she laid a hand on Thomas's sleeve. 'Please, Sir, I have a favour to beg of you. It is my maid, Nellie. She has been with me so long I do not think I can do without her services now. And I will need my own personal maid when I am wed . . . '

'If it pleases you, my dear, it shall be so,' Thomas said with a chuckle. 'And now, enough talk. I deserve a kiss do I not?' He pulled her to him and planted his fleshy lips over hers. This time, she did not try to move away. This was her penance and she would do well to get used to it.

The gown was finished and hung on a hook behind the door of Hester's bedchamber. It was beautiful. The sunlight glinting off the water glanced through the open window, causing the silk to ripple and shine like the reflection of the sky in the river on a summer day. But Hester could take no pleasure in it.

Nellie was delighted. 'Oh, Mistress Hester, it's lovely,' she said stroking the soft silk, her eyes dreamy. 'Do you think I shall have such a gown when Dan and I are wed?' she asked.

Hester smiled. 'You shall have this one when I am done with it. Besides, it matters not what you wear. Dan loves you, and he will see the girl he loves, not what she is wearing.'

Nellie's eyes were dreamy. 'Oh, I wish it could be soon.'

'Dan must become established in his trade so that he can support a wife. And, I, being selfish, wish it would be longer before you will leave me.' She took Nellie's hand in hers. 'I cannot tell you how pleased I am that you will be coming with me to my new home. Truth to tell, it is a daunting prospect to leave my father's house and go among strangers.'

'I confess I am somewhat nervous too,' Nellie said.

Hester sat down on the side of her bed. 'In a way I wish you were staying here. I do not know how my father will manage when I am gone. He is in such low spirits since the loss of his workshop.'

Although Charles had lost his livelihood, he had managed to hold on to the tools of his trade and the family still had somewhere to live. The house on the bridge had belonged to Elizabeth's family and was safe from the bailiffs.

Hester had hoped that her father would manage to find work with one of the larger companies of leatherworkers as Dan had done. But he showed little inclination to try and had slumped into a lethargy greater than when his wife and child had died a year ago. She was worried about him but did not know what to do.

As they went downstairs to prepare food for the family, Nellie giggled. 'I do not know why you are so concerned about the Master,' she said. 'I believe he will be well cared for.'

'What do you mean?'

'Why, Mistress Hester, have you not seen the way Mistress Blake looks at him lately? She anticipates his every word and her eyes light up when he enters the room.'

Hester had been so wrapped up in worry about her father and misery at the prospect of her marriage that she had not noticed her aunt's changed manner. Now that Nellie had brought it to her attention, she realised that Mary smiled more often lately and she had regained the old spring in her step.

'Do you think they will wed, Mistress?' Nellie asked.

The idea of her father re-marrying

took some getting used to, but on reflection Hester realised that it would be good for both of them. Mary had been a widow for many years and she had been devoted to Elizabeth. She would not try to take her place, but would offer Charles comfort in his declining years.

'I have not thought about it,' she answered Nellie now. 'But if my father wishes to re-marry, he will have my blessing.'

When Mary returned from the market, Hester noticed that her father, who had been hunched over the fire, glanced up and smiled warmly. He stood up and took the basket from her hand, gesturing her to sit beside him.

Nellie took the basket from him and she and Hester exchanged a smiling glance. In the kitchen the maid whispered, 'You see, I told you it was so.'

Hester could see that the maid was right. Although grief shadowed Mary's eyes, it was more than affection for her dead cousin's kin that showed in her face. Hester was glad that at last Mary seemed to have accepted the loss of her son and was beginning to look to the future.

If she could find a little happiness with Charles, Hester was content. It helped ease her own pain to know that her father would not be lonely when she left for her married home. And that day would come all too soon, she thought with a sigh.

Despite her determination to try and forget Jonathan and do her duty, Hester could not help thinking back to the happy times with him. She told herself she had indeed accepted he would never return, as her aunt had. But deep down the spark of hope still burned. It was not too late. His ship had been lost, but he could have been rescued. Even now, he could be making his way back to London.

At that very moment, the *Caroline* was rounding the North Foreland and beginning the long tack up the estuary into the lower reaches of the Thames. Captain Jonathan Blake stood on the foredeck, keeping a sharp eye on the helmsman, the lift of the spirits that they all felt on being within sight of home had caused many a seaman to lapse his concentration and Captain Blake knew the dangers of these tidal waters.

He scanned the choppy surface of the sea for the telltale swell that would indicate a hidden sand bar, then looked up at a sky the clear blue of a summer's day. But there was a chill to the wind and he shivered.

Footsteps clattered on the companionway behind him and he turned to greet the newly-promoted mate, Ben Weaver.

'This wind chills my bones,' Jonathan said. 'I shall not be sorry to set off again for the Indies. I have got used to warmer climes.'

Ben laughed, 'I for one am pleased to be home. My good wife will have forgotten what I look like and the babes will be almost full grown.'

Jonathan frowned but did not reply, pretending to be engaged in checking their course. If he had a wife and children waiting for him, he too would be eager to return home, in fact, he would not have left them in the first place. When he had sailed from Falmouth more than a year ago, he had determined that he would make one last voyage before settling on land with the woman he loved.

His fist clenched on the deck rail and a spasm of pain crossed his face. The damned plague. People spoke of God's will but he could not believe that. Some said it was punishment for the evil in their midst. But why should God punish the innocent too?

His beautiful Hester, his mother who had spent her life doing kindness to others, the gentle Elizabeth, and Charles, who had been a second father to him.

Grief and anger had kept him away from home all this time. He had returned to England only once and then stayed in Gravesend, unable to face going to London. This time he could not put it off, for Master Phillips had sent a jollyboat downstream with a message.

The warehouses at Gravesend were full and Jonathan was to take the *Caroline* upriver to Wapping and discharge their cargo there.

The Kent marshes fell behind them and the quays and wharves of Gravesend appeared on their left. After this the river narrowed and Jonathan concentrated on manoeuvring the ship through the craft which thronged the river — merchant ships, flat-bottomed barges, wherries, gigs and jollyboats.

Ben waved a hand at the busy scene. 'Tis a far cry from when we last sailed up the Thames,' he said. 'The city seems to be recovering its fortunes at last.'

When they had sailed this stretch of water a year before, the river bailiffs had stopped every ship and very few were allowed to carry on upriver. Even on his last trip home, there had been fewer boats than usual and the people he had met ashore went about with slumped shoulders and careworn faces. Now, as Ben said, it seemed that the effects of the plague year were diminishing and at last things were returning to normal.

'Will you sail with me again, Ben?' he asked. 'I would not blame you if you wished to spend some time with your family.'

'Much as I love the old woman, you know full well Master Blake, I love the sea more. It is in my blood. I am like a man besotted with ale and I cannot leave it alone. A few days at most, then I shall be off again, whether in the *Caroline* or another ship it matters not.'

'I shall be pleased to have you with me,' Jonathan said. He understood how the man felt. But he knew that if he had a wife and child to go home to, the call of the sea would not drag him away.

'Mayhap we shall have more adventures together, eh?'

'Skirmishes with pirates, becalmed in

the Doldrums, outrunning those cursed Dutchmen in the Channel — yes, we have had adventures aplenty — but I, for one can do without them.'

Ben laughed aloud. 'I saw the gleam in your eye when we left that Dutch frigate behind.' He nodded thoughtfully, the grin fading. 'Yes, there were times when I wondered if I would ever see my dear Nancy and the little ones again. It is indeed, good to be home.'

Looking ahead, Jonathan saw in the distance the gleaming walls of the Tower of London stark against the blue sky. Beyond it and around a bend in the river he pictured the old bridge, the ancient houses crowded along much of its length. Once, the thought would have brought a lift to the heart as he pictured Hester at the window, hoping for a glimpse of his sail in the distance. Now a heaviness enveloped him, like a lump of lead in his belly.

Master Phillips' warehouses came in sight, close to Wapping stairs. There was no wharf here to tie up to and Jonathan ordered the anchor to be thrown over the side. Before it hit bottom and the sails were lowered, gigs had crowded alongside waiting to unload the cargo.

Jonathan sighed and lowered himself over the side into one of the boats. The sooner the cargo was safely ashore and a return shipment loaded, the sooner he could be off again, away from these painful memories.

He climbed the stairs to where Master Phillips waited and followed him down the cobbled lane to his house. Over a tankard of ale and sweetmeats served by a maid, Jonathan filled in the details of the voyage and why it had taken so long. He had already sent a letter from Jamaica by a faster ship telling of the encounter with pirates and the repairs needed to the ship before they could get under way again.

'I had hoped that we would be only days behind the messenger, not months,' he said. 'But we cannot control the weather.'

'Well, you are home safe, Captain

Blake, and the cargo too. Your share will be the greater, since without your expert seamanship, it could well have been lost altogether.'

Jonathan glowed with pride at the man's words. But his pleasure would have been the greater if Hester were here to share the riches he had gained. How could Master Wright have refused to allow them to marry?

Now, he was impatient to be away, to supervise the loading and provisioning of the ship. But politeness kept him in his seat as Master Phillips told him the city's news — how Master Pepys had berated Parliament for their refusal to allocate more funds to the Navy, how the King sported with his paramours at Whitehall, careless of the threat from the Dutch.

'You have doubtless heard, Master Blake, of the disastrous battle a few days since. Twenty warships we lost and now the fleet is laid up in the Medway, leaving our merchant ships vulnerable . . . ' His voice trailed away and he banged the tankard down on the table.

Jonathan sympathised. He had suffered more than one skirmish with the Dutch these past two years.

Master Phillips stood up. 'Well, Captain, I must not detain you. It will be some days before the *Caroline* is to sail again, and I am sure you are longing to see your mother. It is many months since you were last in London, is it not?'

'Did you not hear? My mother perished in the plague. I have no-one now.' Suddenly Jonathan made up his mind. He had not wanted to go anywhere near the Wrights old home, but now he felt a longing to see the old house again. He could not bear the thought of Hester and her family buried in a common grave. But he would go to the church and light a candle for them.

While there, he could seek out the Reverend Taylor, who had been a good friend to Mary and the Wrights. He hoped that the priest had been there to comfort their last hours.

Bidding Master Phillips a hasty

farewell, Jonathan hurried away. His steps took him through the maze of warehouses that were the lifeblood of the port of London, and past the Tower which had been palace and prison these past five hundred years.

He passed the house of Thomas Latham, a large rambling mansion with overhanging jetties and stout timbers which backed on to the river. Alongside ran a narrow cobbled street that led to the wharves and warehouses that housed the merchant's wealth.

Jonathan recalled his last encounter with Thomas at the time of the plague. He had not recognised him at first, encased as he was in the mask which many wore in an attempt to escape the plague. The memory of what the merchant had told him sent a shudder through him and he hurried on.

At the end of London Bridge he paused, reluctant to confront the past. After a few moments he turned away and made his way towards the church of St Giles.

8

It was a fine autumnal day, that first Saturday in September when Hester woke to the realisation that this was her wedding day and there was no escape. She stood in a daze as Mary and Nellie helped her to dress in the wedding gown of pale blue silk with its high lace collar.

Her heart thumped painfully as she approached St Giles' Church. She took her father's arm and started down the aisle, willing her steps to remain steady and her hands to cease their trembling. The church door clanged shut behind her, shutting out the sunlight, and she finally accepted that nothing could stop the wedding now.

When Thomas turned to her with a smile of triumph on his fleshy face, Hester lowered her eyes and kept them downcast throughout the ceremony, whispering her responses through a dry throat. She hardly realised it was over until she stood at the lych gate.

Friends and well-wishers crowded round and she tried to smile. She heard a voice call her name and she turned, hope flaring in her breast. 'Jonathan?' she whispered. Was it really him?

She started forward, careless of her new husband's hand on her arm. Only the vicious grip of his fingers on her wrist brought her to a halt and she bit her lip as his hot breath hissed in her ear. 'Have a care, Mistress Latham. You are my wife now and I'd not take it lightly were you to shame me before my friends.'

Hester only just managed to bite back her angry retort. As Thomas's wife she knew she must obey him. She lowered her eyes, but not before she had cast one last longing look to where Jonathan and his mother were deep in conversation. She saw Mary's stricken face, heard Jonathan's gasp of disbelief, and then her husband was ushering her into his carriage and ordering the servant to drive on.

Jonathan had arrived at St Giles' a few moments before the church doors opened and the wedding party emerged. He approached the knot of people by the lych gate and heard the sound of music issuing from the building.

'I wish to speak to the rector,' he told a bystander, 'but it seems he is engaged at present. Is it a wedding?'

The woman gave a toothless grin. 'It is the merchant Master Latham who is marrying today.' She sighed. 'You should see the bride — a prettier maid there never was.'

A man nearby spoke up. 'Would that I were a widower and could persuade so sweet a maid to wed me,' he said amid coarse laughter.

Just then the doors opened and the crowd surged forward to greet the couple and to touch their sleeves for luck. Jonathan had no wish to confront Thomas and he stood to one side. When they had gone he would speak to the priest.

The bride was turned away from him, eyes modestly downcast, but there was something in the tilt of her head that drew him to her. 'Hester?' he whispered, not daring to believe. Then, as his eyes widened in disbelief mingled with anger, more loudly. 'Hester — it is you?'

He saw the hatred in Thomas Latham's eyes, the cruel grip on Hester's wrist and he lunged forward. A hand restrained him and he gazed into his mother's face. Master Wright stood nearby.

The shock on their faces mirrored that on his own and, even as his own body started to tremble, he saw his mother's legs begin to buckle.

His arms came round her as she swooned and when he looked back Hester and her new husband had gone.

He and Charles helped Mary back into the church so that she could recover.

Kneeling at her side, Jonathan chafed her cold hand. 'Mother, I thought you

were dead. Master Latham said . . . '
His voice trailed away and he looked up
at Master Wright. 'He told me you had
all perished in the plague. Why would
he say such a thing? I don't understand.' He shook his head.

Charles' face was grim. 'I fear I am
somewhat to blame — although, my
boy, it is so long since we had news of
you that we had given you up for dead.
Your poor mother has been grieving for
nigh on a year.'

'What do you mean — you are to
blame?' Anger flared in Jonathan's eyes
and he gripped Charles' arm. 'Explain
yourself, sir.'

'When Thomas Latham sought permission to court my daughter, he asked
if there was not some young man who
had taken her fancy. I told him she had
an affection for you but that you would
be in no position to wed for many a
year.'

He looked away, moistening his lips.
'I thought a rich merchant would be a
better match for my daughter than a

poor seaman. When we did not hear from you, it seemed right to allow them to be betrothed.'

Mary stirred in her seat and gazed at Jonathan, love shining from her eyes. 'My son — restored to me. I hardly dare believe it. We were told that the *Caroline* was lost with all hands.'

'Who told you this?' he asked, helping her to her feet. Then, seeing her expression, he said, 'No. Do not tell me — I believe it must have been Master Latham.'

He was still angry, but now his anger was directed at Thomas.

'It seems there is no end to the man's treachery in order to gain what he desires. Well, he shall answer to me.'

He strode towards the church porch, but Charles barred his way.

'You can do nothing, Jonathan. Think about it. They are wed — and those whom God has joined, no man can put asunder.'

Mary laid a hand on his arm. 'Master Wright speaks truly, son. You must try to forget Hester — it was not meant to be.'

'Tell me she went to him willingly and I will be back to the sea and never come nigh her again,' Jonathan said.

Charles evaded the question. 'It is a good match, she will want for nothing,' he said defensively. 'Maybe it is better if you return to your ship now.'

Jonathan started to walk away but Mary called him back. 'Do nothing in haste, son. Wait at Master Wright's house until I return. We must join the newlyweds at their home, but I must spend some time with you before you sail away again. You must have many a tale to tell of your journeyings abroad and I want to hear everything that has happened to you.'

'I am the captain of the *Caroline* now,' he said proudly, turning to Charles with a hint of defiance in his voice. 'I can assure you I am now in a position to take a wife. If Hester had truly loved me, she would have waited.'

'But we thought you were dead. The

poor girl grieved for many months, as we all did. Would you wish her to remain a spinster all her life?' Mary asked.

Jonathan did not answer and Charles took Mary's arm. 'Come, my dear. We must away to Master Latham's house. I cannot be absent from my only daughter's wedding feast — much as I might wish things were different. But we must all make the best of it.'

Mary bade her son farewell, promising that she would speak to Hester alone, and explain what had kept him from London all these months.

She and Charles walked away and he stood watching until they were out of sight. But he did not go to the house on London Bridge. After a few moments he followed them towards Thames Street and the house of the merchant.

9

When the carriage reached the mansion in Thames Street, Hester's head was still reeling. She hardly noticed Mary and her father's absence as Thomas led her into the great hall where tables had been set out, groaning with rich food and drink, ready for the wedding feast.

In the carriage Thomas had whispered in her ear, his arm around her, but she dared not shrink away. She tried not to let him see how the shock of Jonathan's reappearance had affected her. He knew that she was fond of her cousin, but she feared his cruel reaction if he should realise how much she loved him.

The revelry got under way and Hester allowed her glass to be refilled often, hoping the unaccustomed wine would deaden her senses. As toast after toast was drunk to the bride and groom, her new husband became louder and more boisterous. His lewd jests were greeted with laughter by his cronies and many remarks were made concerning the bride's maidenly blushes.

As the drunkenness increased, Mary approached the high table. 'I think it is time,' she whispered and made a signal to Nellie who hovered in the doorway of the great hall.

Thomas laughed. 'Indeed it is time. I will be along shortly, my dear.' He wagged a finger in Mary's face. 'Do not take too long in your preparations. The groom grows impatient.'

Hester rose from the table, staggering a little, not just from the wine she had drunk, but from the torment of her thoughts. She should be thanking God that Jonathan was alive and well. But all she could think of was that soon she would be sharing a bed with Thomas Latham.

The revellers accompanied the bride with good-natured banter and bawdy suggestions up the wide stairs to the master bedroom. A fire had been lit and the room was bright with many candles. Hester glanced fearfully at the huge four-poster bed, hung with rich tapestries.

She submitted as Nellie helped her disrobe, and slipped a fine fawn nightgown over her head. She sat at the dressing-table while Mary took the pins from her hair and brushed it till it shone in the candlelight.

If only she would say something. But her aunt seemed lost in thought. Hester could bear it no longer and burst into tears. 'Why did he not come back before?' she wept. 'He promised that we would be betrothed and now it is too late.'

Mary comforted her as best she could. 'He was misinformed. He heard that we had all perished in the plague. The poor boy has been crazed with grief this past year. He could have returned when the epidemic was over but he could not bring himself to come back to London. Instead he set off on a long voyage. He has been to the West Indies and has returned as Captain of his ship.' Mary could not kept the note of pride from her voice and Hester smiled through her tears.

'He always said he would make us proud of him.' She sniffed and wiped her hand across her tear-stained face.

Mary leaned over and kissed her cheek. 'Come, dry your eyes, child. Your husband will be here soon and it would not do for him to see tears on your wedding night — especially if he should guess the cause.' There was a note of warning in Mary's voice and when Hester shook her head in despair she said, 'He is your husband and you must obey him, my dear.'

'I hate him,' Hester muttered. 'It was he who told us that Jonathan was dead. I will never forgive him.'

Her head came up at a sound outside the door. Drunken laughter and ribald comments accompanied Thomas as he was escorted into the chamber.

Mary drew back the bed hangings

and turned back the sheet. Trembling, Hester climbed into the high bed and drew the sheet up to her chin. Mary kissed her brow and Nellie whispered a fond 'goodnight'. Then they were gone, leaving her to await her husband.

Thomas' friends helped him off with his boots, laughing as he almost fell from the chair.

'I hope he is not too drunk to do his duty by his new wife,' one of them said with a lewd cackle of laughter.

Thomas stood up, swaying, and took a step towards the bed, roughly pushing the man away.

'Methinks he is over eager,' another said.

They pulled the rest of his clothes off and helped him on with his nightshirt. The men paused at the door, waiting while the servant tidied away the clothes and extinguished the candles.

When they had left, Thomas leered at her, his face ruby-red in the firelight, his wig askew. 'Alone at last, my pretty.'

He staggered towards the bed and lunged at her.

Determined as she was to try and make the best of things, Hester could not stop herself shrinking away as his foul breath struck her face.

Thomas' grin faded and his eyes narrowed. 'What have we here? A shrinking violet. Where is the little wildcat I so looked forward to taming?' He grabbed her arm and pinched it but Hester did not flinch.

'I am your wife, Sir, and I will do my duty,' she said with a semblance of dignity.

He slipped, clutched at the bed-hangings and fell, sprawling. He made an attempt to pull the sheet away, but his hand pawed uselessly and he began to mumble drunkenly. Hester remained propped against the pillows, her eyes wide in the firelight, afraid to move in case she disturbed him. He began to snore and she allowed herself a small smile. For all his boasting and strutting he was just an old man who could not hold his drink.

She steeled herself to move, to inch away from the sour wine smell on his breath. He murmured something and rolled closer to her, reaching out a hand. Then he gave a loud snort and fell back on the bed. Within seconds he was snoring loudly.

When it seemed certain he would not rouse from his drunken stupor, Hester plucked up the courage to get out of bed. She crept to a chair by the window and sat tensely, dreading Thomas would waken.

Tears trickled down her cheeks as she recalled that fleeting glimpse of Jonathan by the church gate, the cold shock of thinking he was a ghost come to haunt her for marrying Thomas, then the despair at realising he had returned too late. She gazed at the bed where Thomas lay, mumbling and twitching in his inebriated sleep, a gaze filled with hatred for the sorrow and pain he had brought her and her family.

As her aunt helped prepare her for

bed, Mary had told how Thomas had sent Jonathan away, telling him they had all died. And she remembered his cruel words that the *Caroline* had been lost with all hands. How could a man who professed to love her, be so cruel? And how could she live with such a man? She sighed and curled up in the chair and at last, exhausted by the emotional turmoil, she managed to sleep.

★   ★   ★

Hester did not know how long she had slept. She woke suddenly and her eyes went straight to the bed. In the faint glow of the firelight, she saw to her relief that Thomas had not stirred.

She stretched her cramped limbs and stood up, wondering what had disturbed her. The fire was almost out and she felt cold. She fetched a robe and, wrapping it around her, she curled up on the chair again. But she could not get back to sleep.

She started up again when she heard shouts and running footsteps. Surely the revellers had all gone home by now? She looked out of the window and saw a reddish glow in the sky to the east. Was it dawn already — the first day of her new life as Mistress Latham? Then her nostrils caught the acrid smell of smoke and she realised there was a fire nearby.

She watched as the glow grew ever brighter and she began to be a little fearful. From the noises she had heard she was sure the watch had been called out and that soon the fire would be under control. But fire was not something the people of London took lightly.

Among the close-packed alleyways and courts it could spread rapidly. She wondered whether she should try to wake her husband. But the glow in the sky seemed far enough away and she did not think there was any danger as yet.

She knew she should rest but she

could not bring herself to get into bed with Thomas. She stood at the window, watching as the orange and red light grew ever brighter. Was it nearer now? She flung open the window, gasping as the wind almost tore the casement from her hand. The bed hangings danced in the onrush of wind and Thomas stirred and groaned.

But Hester took no notice of him. Her heart thumped and her head was full of a roaring and crackling. Like a huge dragon the fire was raging towards them. She leaned out of the window to cry for help. But there was no-one nearby.

She fancied she could feel the heat now and she trembled, remembering a great fire on London Bridge when she was a child which had destroyed many of the houses near her home.

Why had no-one raised the alarm, she wondered? Surely someone else had heard the commotion? She went to the door to call the servants but there was no reply.

'Nellie, where are you?' she cried. The girl had drunk her fair share of ale and was probably still sleeping, Hester thought. It was up to her to rouse the household.

She descended the wide staircase into the great hall where a few of the wedding guests remained. They were slumped over the table, tankards still in their hands, many snoring loudly. Hester ran amongst them shouting and shaking them to try to alert them to the danger. At last she managed to make them understand what was happening and they stumbled blearily to their feet.

A manservant came downstairs in his nightshirt, barefoot, holding a candle. 'What's amiss?' he asked, rubbing his bleary eyes.

'Fire! fire!' Hester screamed, but her voice was hoarse with shouting.

'Where? What fire?' the man said, gazing round at the great hall.

'Outside — in the street. It will soon be upon us,' Hester said. 'Quickly, help me rouse the household and get everyone out.' He wrestled open the heavy front door and ushered the guests into the street which was now filled with shouting scurrying figures.

No-one had come downstairs and Hester ran back into the rambling old house. She could not believe anyone could sleep through the roar of the flames and the commotion outside. She was not even sure where the servants slept or how many there were.

She bounded up the stairs and as long a wide gallery until she found another staircase which led to the attic. Up here the smell of smoke was stronger and she was sure she could feel the heat. She coughed as the smell of burning pitch from the chandler's next door mingled with the smell of ash and caught in her throat.

At last she found Nellie's room. The maid was awake, staring with frightened eyes, while the other servants milled around, uncertain what to do. Hester took her arm and pushed her in the direction of the stairs. 'Wait for me outside,' she ordered.

'But, Miss, I cannot leave you,' Nellie cried, clutching at her hand.

'I have to make sure all are safe. Go on,' Hester said.

Nellie stumbled downstairs in the wake of the servants and Hester was about to follow them when she remembered Thomas. Has he woken and managed to escape?

Once she was sure the servants had left, Hester returned to the bed-chamber. The window was still open and she could hear the roar of the flames, feel the hot wind on her face. But Thomas still sprawled in his drunken stupor.

She tried to rouse him, punching his shoulder and slapping at his face when shaking did no good. At last he opened his eyes and stirred. 'Thomas, you must wake up. Please wake up,' she begged.

He stretched out his arms and slurred, 'Are you so eager for your husband my pretty one?'

She pushed his hands away, sobbing

in frustration. 'There is a terrible fire, Thomas. We must get out of the house.'

Crimson sparks danced past the window, fanned by the strong wind and Hester expected the roof to catch at any moment. The crash of falling timbers brought Thomas fully awake. Pushing Hester aside, he leapt out of bed and ran out of the room, calling for the servants.

When there was no reply he roared in fury. 'Where are the lazy sots? Why do they not answer? They must get my goods out of the warehouse.'

'The servants have all fled, Sir,' Hester said, pulling at his sleeve. 'And we must go too. The roof may fall in at any moment.'

To her relief he went down the stairs, but instead of going out of the front door, he ran towards the back of the house. Hester followed him through a small door which gave on to the small yard separating the mansion from the warehouse.

'The Indian carpets promised to the

Duke must be saved or I will be ruined,' he cried, plunging into the smoke-filled warehouse. He began pulling at the bales and chests as if he alone could save his precious goods.

Fear clutched at Hester's heart as the heat intensified and her breath was almost sucked from her body. But even her hatred of Thomas could not stop her making one last attempt to persuade him of the danger.

'Please, Sir, come away. We will both be killed.'

But he shook her off impatiently and continued pulling at the bales, seeming to be unaware of the danger. She watched helplessly until he turned on her savagely. 'Fetch men, girl. Hurry, or all will be lost.'

She saw that her pleas were no use and she turned away, intending to fetch help. But she felt herself begin to choke and her knees buckled under her as she succumbed to the smoke.

10

Jonathan paced up and down the narrow street, clenching and unclenching his fists, glancing up at the windows of the Latham house. As the sounds of merry-making grew louder, he was finding it harder to resist rushing inside and confronting the man who had stolen his love.

Part of his anger was directed at Master Wright who had forced his daughter into a loveless marriage. 'How could he do it?' he muttered.

His head told him that marriage was often a business transaction and that since they all believed him dead, it made sense for her father to make sure Hester was well provided for. But to choose such a man.

His anger flared anew as he thought of Thomas Latham's wickedness, picturing his mother's greying hair and lined face. She had aged far more in a year than he would have expected. And what of poor Hester? He had seen the nervous glances at her new husband as they left the church. He had seen, too, the momentary flash of joy as she caught sight of him, quickly quelled when Latham pulled her away.

Darkness had fallen and the sounds of revelry increased. Candles were lit and he saw shadows moving behind the heavy draperies. A light appeared in the window of an upstairs chamber and a knot formed in his stomach at the thought of what was shortly to take place. But there was nothing he could do about it. At last he turned away and walked slowly in the direction of Master Wright's house.

At the end of the bridge he paused, hearing shouts and running footsteps. Looking back, he saw a glow in the sky. There was a fire somewhere but it seemed a long way away. Fires were not uncommon among the close-packed houses to the east of the city. But there were always those who would flock to gawp at a disaster.

He almost turned to go to offer help. After all, it was unlikely he'd get any sleep this night. But his mother was waiting to hear the tale of his voyaging and she would begin to fret if he did not go home soon.

Mary and Charles were alone when he reached the house. He could see at once how it was with them and even in his misery he could be glad for his mother. He had long wished his mother would re-marry. She had been a widow far too long. And, since he intended to return to Gravesend the following day and not return for many a year, it would comfort him to know that she would be cared for in her old age. And with Hester and Nellie gone, Master Wright needed a woman to look after him.

They sat long into the night exchanging their news and Jonathan's fury was like a stone in his belly when he realised how Thomas Latham had tricked them all with his lies.

When Mary got up to fetch them ale, he remarked that they would need to engage another maid to replace Nellie.

Master Wright coughed and looked embarrassed. 'I fear that will not be possible just yet,' he said.

Mary put a hand on Charles' arm and smiled. 'I am quite able to look after our small household — and shall take pleasure in doing so,' she said.

Jonathan did not understand until Master Wright told him how the plague had been only the latest disaster in a string of troubles that had robbed him of his fortune. 'I have only this house and the tools of my trade, so must make shift to start again. My rich clients have all deserted me and I am reduced to making shoes for the poorer classes.'

'What of Dan and young Will?' Jonathan asked.

'I feel badly for them.' Charles sighed. 'They tried so hard to keep the workshop going. It was only their presence that prevented it being looted and their reward is to be turned off.'

Mary returned with the jug of ale and poured for the two men. 'You did your best by them, my dear,' she said.

'I released Dan from his indentures and signed his papers as a journeyman — he had less than a year to go. He is now employed to the north of the city and will probably start up his own business when he has saved sufficient capital,' said Charles.

'And what of Will?'

'I was fortunate enough to be able to transfer his apprenticeship to a saddler whose own apprentice died in the plague. The man has agreed to count the years already served since the boy was learning to work in leather.'

Master Wright stood up and yawned. 'It has been a long day, full of excitement and shocks. I am too old for such doings and must away to my bed.'

Jonathan did not want to go to bed. He knew he would only lie awake thinking of Hester and the impossible situation they were in. Relating the tale of his wanderings to this mother and Master Wright had distracted him, but all the while they were talking, images he did not care to see danced at the back of his mind.

A pounding came at the door and a voice shouted, 'Master Wright, I saw your light and knew you were not abed. Come and see . . . '

Jonathan pulled the door open and the man who stood there gestured wildly. 'A fire — and they say it is spreading fast, coming this way. Those at the other end of the bridge are moving their goods. I advise you to do the same.'

They crowded to the door and looked to the east where the lurid glow that Jonathan had noticed earlier now filled the night sky, becoming brighter even as they stared. Scurrying figures pushing carts trundled across the bridge, their faces etched with panic.

Mary clutched Jonathan's arm. 'What shall we do?'

He glanced at Charles and saw the

same thought echoed in his eyes. 'Hester.'

Without another word, they left the house and hurried towards the end of the bridge and into Thomas Street. As they neared Master Latham's house they could feel the heat and smell the smoke. But worst of all was the noise — a roaring and crackling that drowned out all other sounds.

The wind was stronger now and carried before it sparks and embers that danced like fireflies past them as they broke into a run. But they were too late. Master Latham's house was already on fire. And as they stood, clutching each other in fear, the roof of the mansion collapsed in on itself in a shower of sparks. The chandler's next door was already a smoking heap of rubble, acrid black smoke from the melting tallow swirling towards them, causing them to choke.

At the corner of the street a knot of bystanders, many in their nightshifts, watched the progress of the fire, seeming unable to take their eyes from the awesome spectacle.

Jonathan grabbed one by the arm. 'What of Master Latham's household?' he demanded.

'I know not except that the new mistress roused the household and got the servants out,' he said.

'Is she safe? Where is she?' He swung round frantically, almost knocking over the small figure who stood behind him, tears making white lines in her sooty face.

'Nellie. Thank God. Where is your mistress?' he asked.

Nellie's chest heaved with sobs. 'She saved me, Master Jonathan. But . . . ' She coughed, overcome with weeping.

'Tell me.' Jonathan gripped the girl's arm, resisting the urge to shake her.

'She went back into the house to save Master Latham.'

Mary began to weep and Charles stood helplessly gazing at the ruined houses, careless of the danger from falling timbers and masonry. 'My poor

Hester,' he sobbed.

Jonathan took him by the shoulders and shook him savagely. 'Master Wright, we must do something. Go back to the bridge and fetch a boat. Tell them to bring it alongside the warehouse. They may have tried to escape that way.'

Charles did not move and Jonathan shook him again. 'Go now,' he said. 'Mother, go with him and wait at the house.'

Without waiting for a reply, he plunged towards the ruined house, clambering over the smouldering ruins and hoarsely shouting his loved one's name.

In her dream, Hester could hear someone calling her. It sounded like Jonathan. But Jonathan was dead, wasn't he? Maybe she was dead, too, and they were together again at last, as she had so often prayed they would be.

The voice came again and she stirred, coughing as the smoke caught at her lungs. Her mind cleared and she saw once more the flames leaping towards her, crossing the street to engulf the houses alongside. She raised her head and saw through the thick choking smoke that the piles of bales surrounding her were smouldering from the sparks that had fallen on them.

Had she imagined it? But there it was again. 'Hester, answer me.'

She tried to shout a reply, but her voice was hoarse from the smoke. 'I'm here, Jonathan.' It was a mere whisper and then her eyes closed as she fainted again.

Strong arms lifted her and carried her outside. She stirred as she felt the welcome cool air on her face and smelled the river. She lifted her head and gazed up into the dear face of her beloved.

'Here she is, Master Wright,' the loved voice said.

'Is she hurt?' It was her father.

She looked round but could not see him. They were in the narrow alleyway between the warehouses. Flames were shooting from the roof and, as she watched, they leapt across the gap to the Latham building. She struggled in Jonathan's arms. 'Where is my father? Is he all right?'

Jonathan set her on her feet and pointed to the river where Dan and her father steadied the small boat against the steps. Willing hands helped her down and her father reached up and embraced her with tears in his eyes. 'Thank God you are safe, daughter,' he said.

Hester returned his embrace, and the boat rocked dangerously.

'Sit down, my dear. You will soon be home safe,' Charles said.

She looked up at the narrow wharf. 'Jonathan? Where is he?'

But he had disappeared. She stood up, careless of the waves splashing over the sides of the boat. The riverfront was lit as if it were full day and the water was thronged with craft, as eager to save their goods from the burning warehouses as to save lives. Thomas

Latham's fine mansion and the adjacent houses were now a heap of ash, the warehouses fronting the river wreathed in flames.

Where was Jonathan? Why had he gone back into the burning building?

Charles took her hand and forced her to sit in the stern of the boat. Dan began to row away from the bank.

'Wait,' Hester cried. 'We cannot leave him.'

'It is too dangerous,' Charles said.

But, peering through the smoke, Hester saw a figure appear, staggering under the weight of its burden.

Dan manoeuvred the boat back to the steps and helped Jonathan lift the unconscious figure into it. Charles turned him over and Hester gasped as she recognised the face of her husband beneath the soot and grime. Her hands covered her face and she tried to pray. Tears began to trickle through her fingers when she heard her father say, 'You were too late, my boy. God rest his soul.' He took Hester's hand. 'My poor daughter — a widow before you were scarce a wife,' he said sadly.

'I tried to make him see the danger, but he would not listen. He thought only of saving his goods.' Hester sobbed.

'It was his greed, the need to save his wealth, which killed him,' Charles said. 'Nellie told us you went back into the house for him.'

Hester dried her eyes. 'I hated him, but I could not let him die,' she said.

'You did what you could,' Charles said, trying to comfort her. He turned to Dan. 'There's nothing more we can do. Make for the bridge, lad. Mistress Mary will be afeared something has happened to us.'

Back at the house, Mary made a soothing tisane for them all to drink to counteract the effects of the smoke which had them all hoarse and coughing. Dan had gone out again and returned a few minutes later with Nellie, who burst into tears at the sight of her mistress and would not leave her side.

There was no talk of going to bed for what remained of the night, for they could tell from the noise and stench of smoke that the fire still raged, seemingly out of control.

From time to time one of them would go to the door to see how it progressed and to ask news of one of the streams of people leaving the city for the safety of the south bank.

As the fire neared the end of the bridge they began to make plans to abandon the house. Hester was still weak from her ordeal and lay on the couch where her mother had spent so many hours, while Mary and Nellie began to pack up the more valuable of the household goods.

They had left the body of Master Latham in the boat, tied up to one of the bridge supports. By morning the fire would surely have spent itself and Charles could find a priest and arrange a fitting burial for his son-in-law.

But when dawn finally came there was no end to the nightmare. Ignoring

Nellie's fearful protests, Dan went towards the city to see if his new employer's house had been spared. When he came back, his voice was grim.

'There is nothing left of the church of St Magnus, nor of the houses surrounding it,' he said. 'My master's house is gone and I can only pray he and his family have escaped safely.'

'What of the bridge?' Jonathan asked. The smoke was so dense, it was like a huge grey wall, stretching as far as the eye could see and shutting out the sky.

'The sparks have set some of the houses off, those near the street, but so far we are spared. The wind is blowing away from us, so we should be safe for a while.'

'What are the authorities doing?' Mary asked.

'Nothing at the moment, it seems,' Dan replied grimly. 'I heard that the King had ordered some houses to be torn down to make a firebreak. But the Mayor is saying that he cannot enforce it for no-one will obey him.'

'I suppose the authorities are afraid that they will have to compensate those who lose their houses through their forcible destruction,' Charles said.

'What nonsense,' Jonathan replied. 'They will lose everything in any case if nothing is done.'

*   *   *

For two days the Wright household waited in readiness in case they too should have to flee. Never before had a fire raged so strongly and for so long. When they heard that St Paul's Cathedral, which had stood for hundreds of years, was now a pile of smoking ash, it was as if nothing worse could happen.

Charles hailed a passer-by for more news. 'There will be nothing left of London if this continues,' the man said, his back straining to pull the heavily-laden cart.

A neighbour saw Charles at his door and came towards them. 'There will be no need to flee, Master Wright,' he said. 'I have just heard that the King and Duke of York are ordering the houses in the path of the fire to be blown up with gunpowder. I saw the King himself get down from his horse, take off his coat and begin working alongside the men.'

'Truly — the King himself?' Charles called the news to the others, before turning back to his neighbour. 'Do you really think that will work?' he asked.

'It is working already,' the man said.

Hester heard her father's heartfelt, 'Thank the Lord' and stirred on her couch, where Mary had insisted she still rest.

'Are we saved?' she asked, her throat still hoarse from breathing in the smoke.

Jonathan, who had been sitting at her side, holding her hand, stood up and went to question the man himself. He came back, smiling. 'It is under control at last.'

But although Hester rejoiced that her family were safe and that her father would not lose his home as well as his livelihood, her happiness was short-lived.

The fire was out at last, although a few small pockets smouldered here and there. But work had already begun on clearing the rubble and rebuilding the city.

It was scarcely a week since Hester had left the church on the arm of her new husband, yet so much had happened that it seemed like a lifetime. Her disastrous wedding night was now just a dim memory and now that the danger from the fire was past, her thoughts began to turn to the future.

Despite feeling guilty, she was glad Thomas was dead. As her father had said, she had tried to save him and it was his own greed that had caused his death. Besides, she was young and in love, and the man she cared for had been restored to her. She would not have been human if she had not imagined a rosy future with him.

So it was a harsh blow when he rose

one morning shortly after the fire and told her he was off to Gravesend to see Master Phillips. How could he leave her so soon?

They were alone in the room and he pulled her towards him and kissed her gently. 'My dearest Hester, you know I love you but surely you must see that I cannot stay?'

'Why not? I am no longer married, we can be wed . . . '

'Yes, but not yet. Propriety demands that you must observe a year of mourning. My mother and your father would be immensely hurt if we should go against convention.'

'If that is what you want,' Hester said, pouting.

Jonathan lifted her chin with his finger and smiled. 'You know full well it is not what I want. But don't you think they have suffered enough this past year?' He kissed her again, more passionately this time. 'Besides, our union will be all the sweeter for waiting.'

Hester melted into his arms. She knew that Jonathan spoke the truth and she would prefer to have her father's blessing, even if, as a widow, she no longer needed it.

She returned his kiss and murmured. 'But I do not see why you have to go away. Could you not find employment here in London?'

Jonathan pulled her to him, almost crushing the breath from her body. He groaned as his lips sought hers. 'My dear, sweet, Hester. Surely you see that I must leave? It would be torture to be close to you every day and not be able to . . . '

She blushed and pulled away from him. 'I see what you mean,' she said, straightening his bodice. 'But promise me you will not be away too long.'

He laughed. 'I am only going to Gravesend. If Master Phillips offers me a ship I may have to go straight away. But I will try to come back, before setting off on a long voyage.'

11

When he was gone, Hester returned to her old habit of sitting by the window and gazing downstream, dreaming of her future with Jonathan.

Charles had grudgingly given his blessing, but he still spent many hours bemoaning the fact that all Thomas Latham's wealth had gone up in smoke and that his daughter was once again dependent on her family. It had not mattered when he was a prosperous businessman but now, he worried about her ceaselessly.

Hester tried to reassure him that although she would not be rich married to Jonathan, she would be happy.

Since Dan had lost his livelihood because of the fire, he was now back with the Wrights. Each day he went out looking for work and returned disappointed that he could not find anyone to employ him in the craft he had learned with Master Wright.

Nellie was so pleased to have him living under the same roof again that she did not care.

One day he returned from the city, begrimed and sooty, his clothes smelling of smoke. He clutched a battered metal box under his arm and grinned when Hester and Nellie begged him to tell what he had been up to.

'I have been employed by the city authorities,' he said proudly. 'I have been helping to clear away the remains of the buildings by the river.' He held up the box. 'I found this in the ruins of Master Latham's house. It is yours by right, Mistress Hester.'

'I hope no-one saw you take it, Dan. I would not like you to be accused of stealing,' Hester said anxiously.

'Do not fear, Mistress. The watchman who is on guard to stop the looting knows me well. He bid me bring the box to you.'

Hester placed it on the table. It took

a stout kitchen knife to pry the lock open. The papers were curled and brown but still legible. They were bills of lading and bonds, detailing Thomas' dealings.

Nellie looked disappointed. 'I thought there would be gold coins,' she said 'What use is paper?'

Nellie could not read and Hester explained that they were lists of goods that Thomas had in his warehouse.

'But the goods no longer exist,' Nellie said.

Hester nodded agreement, then picked up the papers again. If what she read was true, Thomas had been far wealthier than she had realised. He owned ships and more warehouses downriver. Hester gasped as she realised she was now a very rich widow. Thomas had no other heirs and all that he owned was now hers.

She had never craved riches for herself and was happier in the little house on London Bridge than she ever would have been as mistress of the

Latham mansion. But with Thomas' wealth she could ensure the wellbeing of those she loved. She could pay off her father's creditors and set him up in a new workshop. Dan could work for him and in time would be able to support a wife.

Hester smiled as she told Nellie her plans and could not wait for Mary and her father to return so they could share the good news.

When Charles came in he sat at the table and perused the papers, refusing to comment until he had verified their contents. At last he sat back and smiled. 'It is true, my dear. You are indeed a rich woman. And you deserve your good fortune.'

Later, Hester was sitting by the fire with Mary, trying to concentrate on her sewing. She was wondering if she really was fortunate, as she remembered Jonathan's words after the fire, when he had renewed his pledge of marriage.

'I always loved you, Hester, and I always will. I could not bear the thought of you being another man's wife and I cannot pretend to be sorry that your husband is dead. I am even less sorry that his fortune has gone, too.'

'Thomas' riches would have been mine, and all that I have is yours, too,' Hester had told him.

'I would not be dubbed a fortune-hunter, nevertheless,' Jonathan had said.

And Hester had not argued. With Thomas' mansion and warehouse burned to the ground, his riches had gone with him and the question did not arise — until now.

Hester resolved that she would not tell him of the change in her fortunes until after they were wed.

Jonathan stretched out his legs to the fire in Master Philips' drawing-room and took a sip of the fine wine. The merchant had greeted him with a firm handshake and a hearty welcome, promising that as soon as a ship was available, he would give him a command.

He had invited Jonathan to dine with him and bring him up to date on news from the capital.

When Jonathan had related the incredible tale of finding his mother and the rest of the household alive after grieving for them so long, the older man could scarce believe it. 'And the young woman, the one you wished to marry — she lives, too?' he asked.

Jonathan nodded, a foolish grin on his face.

'So why are you going off on yet another voyage? Should you not be planning your wedding?'

'She is in mourning so we must wait,' Jonathan said and changed the subject, telling his friend of the great fire, though not of his part in it.

'I knew of the disaster of course,' Master Phillips said. 'Thank God I moved most of my goods away from London when the plague struck. My warehouses there had not been completely re-stocked so I have lost little.'

'Others fared worse I fear,' Jonathan replied.

'Some even lost their lives — Master Latham, I hear, perished in the fire,' Master Phillips said.

'Yes, and all his goods along with him.' Jonathan could not keep the note of satisfaction out of his voice.

'Not all, surely? Like myself, he had taken space alongside the wharves here.'

'You mean that there is something left for his heirs to inherit?' Jonathan asked.

'A great deal, if my knowledge of Master Latham is correct. And who knows what will happen to it, for I'm sure he had no family.'

'He had a wife,' Jonathan said shortly.

'So he finally married the young maid? I did hear something of the sort.'

'The very day of his death,' Jonathan said.

Master Phillips leaned forward in his chair. 'Do not tell me the poor girl died too.'

'She was saved, thank God.'

175

'I see you have more than a passing interest in this matter,' Master Phillips said, comprehension dawning on his face. 'Was this the girl you were to marry?'

Jonathan nodded and buried his face in his wineglass.

'All's well that ends well, then. You will have your bride — and a rich one, too.' Master Phillips chuckled and got up to poke the fire.

Jonathan took his leave and went back to his lodgings, his thoughts awhirl. As he tried to sleep he cursed Thomas Latham and his riches. He had spoken truly when he told Hester he could not marry her if she were rich. He had had his fill of being beholden to others.

When his father died, he had been just a small boy and, although the Wrights had been kind to him and to his mother, he had always resented having to be dependent on them. As he grew older Master Wright had promised him an apprenticeship as a leather-worker. But he wanted to go to sea

— not just for adventure and the chance of riches, but to show that he could make his own way in the world. He would have stayed away too, were it not for his dawning love for the Wrights' daughter. Well, he had proved himself a worthy suitor but it was too late.

When he rose after a sleepless night, his first instinct was to go down to the quay and jump on a ship — any ship that would take him far away. He could not marry Hester yet anyway, and who knew what might happen while he was at sea. A cynical smile twisted his lips.

Master Wright would surely take control of Hester's money and, if his previous lack of success was anything to go by, there would not be much of a fortune left by the time he returned. Then Hester would be only too content as the wife of a humble sea captain.

As he walked down to the quay, breathing in the fresh autumn air, he realised he was doing Hester an injustice. She loved him and would marry him even if he were a pauper. And he knew it would be most unfair to his mother, as well to Hester, if he were to sail away without a word. They had suffered enough by his earlier absence.

At the quayside, a lighter was making ready to go upstream and Jonathan hailed the seaman who was manning the ropes. 'I have to go to London. May I beg passage with you? I will work my way,' he called.

'Come aboard,' the man said.

Jonathan hoped he would not regret his impulse. But he owed it to Hester to explain his decision. When he had made his fortune at sea, he would come back and propose marriage to her as an equal.

With the news that she was a rich woman, Hester realised that she could no longer spend her time day-dreaming by the window. Her riches brought responsibilities and sorting out Thomas' affairs made the time pass more quickly.

There was much to do, for as she worked through the papers in the tin box, she found that her husband had fingers in many pies. He had employed many people and they had to be found and paid off, for with the house and warehouse gone there was no need of servants.

She turned to her father for help. 'Surely Master Latham employed an agent to deal with his affairs?' she said.

'I think not. He was not a trusting man and he preferred to keep his business to himself,' Charles replied. 'But you will need an agent. We must find a suitable man for the job.'

'Could you not do it, Father?'

Charles shook his head. 'What do I know of trading and merchandise? I am well versed in leather craft but know little of finance — as you well know.'

Hester laid a hand on his arm. 'Father, the loss of your business was no fault of yours. And now you have the chance to start anew.'

But he would not be persuaded.

Hester did not want to entrust her affairs to a stranger and asked Mary's advice.

'My son would do the job excellently,' she said. 'If you can persuade him to give up seafaring, I would be so happy. I dread him going away again and having to endure the anxiety and uncertainty of his return.'

'Why did I not think of it? When we are married, the business will be his anyway.'

'You must be careful how you approach the matter,' Mary warned. 'My son is a proud-man.'

A little later that day when Hester was still poring over her husband's papers, a shadow darkened the door. Jonathan stood there and she leapt up, running to him and raising her face for his kiss.

But his smile was grim. 'We have much to discuss, Hester,' he said.

'We have indeed.' She pulled him over to the table, showing him the papers and telling him of her plans. Her excitement faded when he showed no reaction.

'What is amiss?' she asked. But she knew the answer. It was his stupid pride. She should have obeyed her first impulse and keep the news of her fortune to herself.

She swept the papers on to the floor. 'Jonathan, I understand how you feel. Do you not think I had those same feelings when my father all but sold me to a rich man?'

'It is not the same for a woman,' Jonathan muttered.

'How so? Do you not think I have my pride also?' Her spurt of anger faded and she sank into a chair, covering her face with her hands. She would not cry, she thought. She had shed tears enough this past year and more. She swallowed and looked up at Jonathan who stood with his hands hanging helplessly at his sides.

'I love you, Jonathan,' she said. 'It was my love for you and the love I thought you felt for me that helped me

181

through the dark months. My mother and my baby brother died, my father lost his livelihood, I believed you were dead, and on top of all that I was forced to marry a wicked, lecherous old man.' Her voice broke. 'But through it all, I gained comfort from the knowledge that I had been loved by a good man, even though I had lost him.'

'Hester, my love. Do not cry.' Jonathan was at her side, holding her in his arms.

She looked into his blue eyes, tears shining on her lashes. 'When I realised you were alive, it was the happiest moment of my life, even though I was on my way to that man's house as his wife. I felt I could endure anything so long as you were safe.'

Jonathan kissed her tenderly. 'I do not deserve such selfless love,' he said. 'But I thank God for it. I will make it my life's work to keep you safe and happy.'

'And you will work alongside me, and

use our riches for the good of others?'
Hester asked.

'Whatever you wish my love.'

Hester snuggled deeper into his arms with a sigh of content. And Jonathan felt that at last he truly had come home.

THE END

TO LOVE AGAIN

Catriona McCuaig

Jenny Doyle had always loved her brother in law, Jake Thomas-Harding, but when he chose to marry her sister instead, she knew it was a love that had no future. Now his wife is dead, and he asks Jenny to live under his roof to look after his little daughter. She wonders what the future holds for them all, especially when ghosts of the past arise to haunt them . . .

FINDING THE SNOWDON LILY

Heather Pardoe

Catrin Owen's father, a guide on Snowdon, shows botanists the sites of rare plants. He wants his daughter to marry Taran Davies. But then the attractive photographer Philip Meredith and his sister arrive, competing to be first to photograph the 'Snowdon Lily' in its secret location. His arrival soon has Catrin embroiled in the race, and she finds her life, as well as her heart, at stake. For the coveted prize generates treachery amongst the rivals — and Taran's jealousy . . .